WHY ARE WE IN VIETNAM?
by NORMAN MAILER

"Touchdown! Knockout! . . . A brilliant piece of writing. . . . In the middle of his important and problematic career, this book shows how superbly he can sense and write."
—*Newsweek*

"Some of the finest writing Mailer has done in a long time. . . . It is impossible to walk away from this novel without being sharply reminded of the fact that Norman Mailer is a writer of extraordinary ability."
—*Chicago Tribune* and *Washington Post (Book World)*

"A shattering social commentary. . . . The book is a tour de force, a treatise on human nature, society and war in flip disguise."
—*Dallas News*

BOOKS BY NORMAN MAILER
AVAILABLE IN BERKLEY MEDALLION EDITIONS

THE DEER PARK

ADVERTISEMENTS FOR MYSELF

THE PRESIDENTIAL PAPERS

NORMAN MAILER

WHY ARE WE IN VIETNAM?

A Novel

A BERKLEY MEDALLION BOOK
Published by G. P. Putnam's Sons
Distributed by Berkley Publishing Corporation

TO MY FRIENDS

Roger Donoghue
Buzz Farbar
Mickey Knox
Norman Podhoretz
Cy Rembar
  and
Jose Torres

Copyright © 1967 by Norman Mailer

G. P. PUTNAM'S-BERKLEY MEDALLION EDITION,
MAY, 1968
2nd Printing, December, 1970
3rd Printing, December, 1971
FOURTH PRINTING

SBN 425-01557-2

G. P. Putnam's Sons
200 Madison Avenue
New York, N.Y. 10016

Berkley Publishing Corporation
200 Madison Avenue
New York, N.Y. 10016

BERKLEY MEDALLION BOOKS ® TM 757,375

Printed in the United States of America

★

INTRO BEEP 1

★

Hip hole and hupmobile, Braunschweiger, you didn't invite Geiger and his counter for nothing, here is D.J. the friendLee voice at your service —hold tight young America—introductions come. Let go of my dong, Shakespeare, I have gone too long, it is too late to tell my tale, may Batman tell it, let him declare there's blood on my dick and D.J. Dicktor Doc Dick and Jek has got the bloods, and has done animal murder, out out damn fart, and murder of the soldierest sort, cold was my hand and hot.

Well, now, friends and lovers, that means you out there in all that implosion land, dig into this

—no such thing as a totally false perception. Have you ever contemplate? Listen, dig, Edison says—quote this from McLuhan—*"I start with the intention to increase the speed of the Atlantic Cable, but when I've arrived part way in my straight line I meet with a phenomenon, and it leads me off in another direction and develops into a phonograph."* And that's how Miles Davis was born. Bangalore, don't snore—here's the bulge: Edison was hip, baby, the way you make it is on the distractions. Leave a little of your shit behind each time, that's charity for all. There is probably no such thing as a totally false perception. Por ejemplo, I say Christ is in this toothpaste tube. Duba doo, duba duba doo—there has to be some grain of true. By gum, man, bite on D.J.'s Texas dick—America, this is your own wandering troubadour brought right up to date, here to sell America its new handbook on how to live, how to live in this Electrox Edison world, all programmed out, Prononzo! (this last being the name King Alonso gave to the Spanish royal condom.) Well, Huckleberry Finn is here to set you straight, and his asshole ain't itching, right? so listen to my words, One World, it's here for adolescents and overthirties—you'll know what it's all about when you and me are done, like the asshole belonged to Egypt, man, and the penis

was the slave of the Hebes and the Brews, for they got it girdled with a ring of blood fire, and the nose was the Negroes, for they split it. Now, remember! Think of cunt and ass—so it's all clear. We're going to tell you what it's all about. Go go, Dr. Jek tell the folk, we're here to rock, the world is going shazam, hahray, harout, fart in my toot, air we breathe is the prez, present dent, and God has always wanted more from man than man has wished to give him. Zig a zig a zig. That is why we live in dread of God. Make me another invention, Edison. Bring in the electric come machine. Do you know I think there's a tape recorder in heaven for each one of us? and all the while we're sleeping and talking and doing our daily acts, bonging the gong, blasting the ass, chewing the milch, milking the chintz, and working the jerk, why there is that tape recorder taking it all down, this is D.J. broadcasting from Texas, from Dallas, Big D in Tex, and listen children to your old dear ma, ever notice how blood smell like cunt and ass all mix in one, but rotten, man, the flesh all rotten like meat and fish is biting each other to death, and Death where is your gates, Mother Fucker, are they hot? Big ass tomb, big ass tomb, the fish are in the fireplace and the nerve's begun to sing, make it cool, D.J., make it cool.

CHAP ONE

Well, now," said Mrs. Jethroe, the mother of this extraordinary late adolescent on the fast receding previous page, the one who calls himself D.J. (if you recalled) "well, now," said she, "what am I going to do with Ranald? He's as obscene as a barmaid and just as barmy. The boy needs to be spanked. I would just as soon spank a puma. He's evil," said Mrs. Jethroe to her psychiatrist, who is a Jewish fellow, nothing other, working his ass off in Dallas, which means so to speak that he must spend eight to ten clammy periods of fifty minutes each listening to Dallas matrons complain about the sexual habits of their husbands, all ex hot rodders, hunters, cattlemen, oil riggers, corporation gears and insurance finks, zap! Well, like every one of these bastards (as Mrs. Jeth—call her Death-row Jethroe—might say when her breath is big! like the bottom of a burnt-out bourbon barrel) well, every one of these bastards has the sexual peculiarities of red-blooded men, which is to say that one of them can't come unless he's squinting down a gunsight, and the other won't produce unless his wife sticks a pistol up his ass— that man is of course a cop. If the psychiatrist wasn't such a fink and such a nice Jewish fellow type as to be working for the general good and wheel of society, and if he wasn't afraid of drilling a little career-and-cancer piss right into the heart of Texas, he would write this book about the ejaculatory jump habits of cops, big ass Southern redneck cops all bullwhipped and bull-shitted up into putteez, son, they come more ways—I froth at the mouth, said the killer, but don't think it's spit. Well, what's to say, D.J.'s mother, Death-row Jethroe, is the prettiest little blonde you ever saw (looks like a draw between young Katherine Anne Porter and young Clare Boothe Luce, whew) all perfume snatchy poo, appears thirty-five, is forty-five, airs, humors, curl to her mouth, half Texas ass accent, half London wickedness, trill and thrill, she's been traveling around the world, Heartache House in Bombay and Freedom House in Bringthatpore, shit, she's been getting cunt-tickled and fucked by all the Class I Dongs in Paris and London, not to mention the upper dedicated pricks of Rome and Italy while her hus, big daddy Rusty Jethroe, is keeping up the corporation end all over the world including Dallas, Big D, Tex. That's some end, son, Big N we call it. Mum's first name is Alice. They found her vagina in North Carolina and part of her gashole in hometown Big D. Why? Why was her parts metaphorically blasted? Because, man, she used a dynamite stick for a phallus. You try that sometime for lots of hymen. D.J.'s father, big Daddy, old Rusty, has got the dynamite. He don't come, he explodes, he's a geyser of love, hot piss, shit, corporation pus, hate, and heart, baby, he blasts, he's Texas willpower, hey yay!

Does this idyll of family life whet your curiosity, flame your balls, or sour your spit? Don't argue, Alice Hallie Lee Jethroe is speaking to her Doc, Clam Fink, the Texas Jew, actually his name is Leonard Levin Fichte Rothenberg, pronounced by all big mind Texans as Linnit Live'n Fixit Rottenbug.

"Well, now Lionhard," says Hallelujah Death-row, D.J.'s sweet blond mother to Dr. Fixit, that little ole rottenbug, "will you jes take a fix on what dear Ranald has to say about everything? It's enough to make a mother wipe up Aunt Jemima's puke. For I love him like a jewel even if he is a thief. But he's out of his mind. Poor sad little fellow. He's so delicate and beautiful even if he is barmy as a barmaid."

"Hallie, let's adjust our sense of the real," says Dr. Hebrew Hairy. "Ranald's delicacy and beauty are memory engravings, perhaps are chromosomal etchings, RNA, DNA, RNA, DNA, one for the left eye, one for the right."

"RNA, DNA, RNA, DNA," says Hallelujah.

"The facts," says Fichte, "are these: Your son, Ranald, is six feet one at the age of eighteen, and is considered highly attractive by his social compeers, as well as mean and vicious."

"He read the Marquis de Sade at the age of fifteen."

"And the drug addict William Burroughs, whom personally I can't see as a talent, I mean give me a hot pastrami sandwich, is now his hero."

"Do you mean the Hot Pastrami, Live'n Fixit?" asks Hallelujah.

"No, sir, I mean William Burroughs. Adjust your sense of the real, Alice Hallie Lee Jethroe, the time has come to program out your attitudes.

I saw Ranald at your request, he was recalcitrant, charming, gracious, anti-Semitic, morally anesthetized, and smoldering with presumptive violence, a host of incense, I mean incest fixes, murder configurations, suicide sets, disembowelment diagrams and diabolism designs, mandalas! Face into the eye of the real, Hallelujah, he's a humdinger of a latent homosexual highly over-heterosexual with onanistic narcissistic and sodomistic overtones, a choir task force of libidinal cross-hybrided vectors."

"He has high-breed vectors all rights," says Hallelujah, "he's got the cunningest ancestry, in fact, cause we're on my mother's side from the Norloins."

"New Orleans?"

"Yis, from Norlins, the Norlins Frenchy Montesquious and the Bat Fartsmotherers." But seeing that Levin Fichte is living on her word, she just knocks over a bottle of one of his urine specimens, adieu albumen! and says, "Mon Doo Ginsberg, you're sure full of shit for a doctor, don't y'know there are no fine Southern families called Fartsmotherer? Lord knows we ain't that fucking stupid, why even British county stock wouldn't be called Fartsmotherer, maybe Assknocking, but not the other, you can't analyze me Living Fichte if you don't know things like that, oh poo I wish you was an Italianate Jew, all earthy and Levantine and suave and had a cunt-tickler of a mustache, instead of your clammy cold Lithuanian brow, what are you, a Talmud hokum? speak up, ass, I just wish you was good enough to kiss my sweet perfumed powdered old pooty-toot, hey Linnit? am I getting out my egressions now?"

"I would not call them aggressions so much as identity crises," said Linnit.

"Oh, poo, let me tell you about the Montesquious. Half-Portuguese, half-French, all that hot crazy blood packed one-quarter into me, for the other half of mah mother was just straight Arkansas mule, the Mulies, why they the richest family in Arkansas then, hot out of Peezer, Arkansas, and they used rat paper for tar paper on the Chic Sale, that's how benighted was their latrine, army folk of course, the MacArthurs used to kiss their ass. And my daddy, well he was just a lover of a husband to my ma, and he must have had a dick on him like a derrick, do I shock you, Dr. Jew?"

"To my cornplasters."

"Oh, Linnit, you'll be the death of me yet. Listen to this old hen cackle. Well, Daddy was Indian for sure, and he had a personal odor like hot rocks in the sun which is in me all mixed

13

with the fine sauces of Franco-Portuguese Montesquiou rut—I mean you should smell my armpits, noxious to some, a knockout to others, I keep them perfumed of course, we want no barmaid's fatal scent on Hallie Jethroe, so I wash, Dr. Rothenberg, three times a day, I don't want nothing but a soupçon of my good sweet crazy full-blooded woman's scent on the breeze off my knees, just enough for to keep the breed alive, talk of high-breed vectors, well, my own sweet husband, Big Daddy, David Rutherford Jethroe Jellicoe Jethroe, *Rusty*, is just as high breed as you want, I can't even follow Rusty's family, they're all marshals, and bastards and cowboys, and one desperado, and one railroad tycoon, and one professor at Harvard, first Texas professor they ever had in Upper Clam City, near Clamsville, which is what I call Harvard, now Linnit, you're a Harvard man, tell me straight and clear what I am going to do with Ranald, he's insane, that boy, and he looks just like George Hamilton the actor, who I think is Instant Heaven, he's so brood-looking, yes, there's something Hebrew about Ranald, he's so big and dark and mysterious for eighteen, and he goes all the way back to Egypt you just know unlike you, dear Jew, you Talmud hokum, you clammy Have-it grit, I suppose I now have to pony up my fifty dollars for the hour."

"Madame, you owe me eleven hundred and fifty."

"You'll have to bust a nut to get it, Rottenbug."

"I'll torture you, I love torturing gentile females. All that white buttermilk flesh. Yum, yum. Yum, yum, yum."

Hey, hey, they really talk that way? That little blond lady, Hallie—perfume and powder on the poo—she talk that way? And Rottenbug going yum yum yum—is he out of his fucking skull? Wait and see. Nobody's got any OK patience any more, just cannibals asking for chocolate on their stick—how the hell do you know what Hallie's saying to Linnit and Fixit saying back? Wait and see? You know what they're doing. They're talking about Tex, Tex Hyde, Gottfried "Texas" Hyde Junior, that's D.J.'s best friend, and know what, get that drop of cream off your jeans before you grow hair in your hand, this is the pitch, Tex is half-German and half-Indian on his father's side, Redskin and Nazi all in one paternal blood, and his mother, well, bless his mother, Tex Hyde's mother is jes old rawhide Texas ass family running back thru fifty-two shacks where in each shack the beans in the pot have been stuck on blacky inside side of the pot for six weeks—those beans look like gravel, Marshal Bean—yeah, Tex's mother runs fifty-two shacks right back to the Alamo where all old saddlesore real Texas ass families run back to, why lick the scab on LBJ's knee if one-tenth of all the Dallas ass families that go back to the Alamo was really there, they'd have all drowned in shit they were so congested and Santa Ana could have thrown his marijuana seed on the top and there'd be a forest of hemp now right in the heart of Texas. Which is a favorite theory of the voice you hear now submitted which is that the best hash and cannabis is grown on fertilizer of human shit, who is there to disprove on honest man's folklore?

Well, Tex Hyde, he's a mother fucker, sell you pot was grown on human shit, and he nothing but D.J.'s best friend. And they are terrible together. Listen to Halleloo. Her tone is full of hell right now, Line It With Hot Bugs is shifting in horror in his seat, cause Halleloo is talking in her bitchy boozy voice which means don't come near unless you can steer your prick like a whip and French tickler all in one, worm! us women know which man has got the spring and who and which is the unfortunate dead ass, here is her words, "Tex Hyde is the son of an *undertaker,*

16

I mean think of that, a Montesquiou Jellicoe
Jethroe a-whopping around with a Kraut mortician's offspring, and all that bastard Indian
Hyde blood in the background, firewater and
dirty old Engine oil, Indians unless they're de-
scended from my daddy's line, and never you
mind what it was, don' ask if it's Navaho,
Apache, or any of those Jew shit questions, you
anthropologist manqué, you fuckless wonder
listening to the sex'l habits of all us mule-ass
Texans, ought to get your ears wiped out Dr.
Fink Lenin Rodzianko whateva your name is,
an Indian don't tell the secret of his name in a
hurry to strangers like you, Clam Grits from
Harvard Square, why, honey, that Tex Hyde
don't have Eenyen blood like my daddy and my
Rusty's daddy's daddy, no, it's just the sort of
dirty vile polluted cesspool Eenyen blood like
Mexican—you know just a touch of that Latin
slicky shit in it, vicious as they come, and mated
up, contemplez-vous, to fatty Bavarian oonshick
and poonshick jawohl furor lemme kiss your dirty
socks my leader, can you imagine? the filthiest
of the Indians and the slimiest of red hot sexy-
ass Nazis fucking each other, mating and breed-
ing to produce Tex Hyde who grows up in his
daddy's big booming business which is stuffing
corpses and doing God knows what to their little old

pithy bowels and their dropped stomachs and whatever else corpses got which must be plenty or why pay thousands of dollars for a funeral unless it's a fumigation, hey Tonto? and that boy growing up there comes out like a malevolent orchid in a humus pile, or a black panther, that's what he is, black panther with all his black panther piss, I'm dreaming of him, Linnit, and so is my son, the black puma, he's got my son who's just as beautiful as George Hamilton and more clean-cut swearing by him, the puma and the panther, I think they took the vow of blood, cut their thumbs and ran 'em around the rim of some debutante's pussy, after the way these kids now live there ain't much left for them but to gang fuck tastefully wouldn't you say, speak up, Linnit."

"Now, Hallie, I know you're not going to listen to me."

"But I am, my dear. I fully intend to, Linnit?"

"Yes, milady."

"Tell me I've been ladylike. I know I haven't. I know I've been outré and spouting great clouds of baloney from inner space, I mean you might think my language was the proper vocabulary for a roughneck or a driller, but I adore you, Linnit, cause you got a kind Jewish heart and

I always said when Hitler killed the Jews, half the kindness went out of the world."

"Now tell me he shoulda killed the other half."

"Heh heh, heh heh. Gallows humor, Linnit."

"Hallie, are you saying you've got to separate those boys?"

"I know, I know. But they're stuck to each other like ranch dogs in a fuck. Hunting together, playing football together on the very same team, riding motorcycles together, holding hands while they ride, studying karate together, I bet they can't even get their rocks off unless they're put-putting in the same vaginal slime, I hope at least Ranald has got the taste and sentiment to be putting it in the young lady's vagina rather than going up her dirt-track where old Tex Hyde belongs (after all those bodies he helped his fat growing rich daddy embalm, baby) but kiss the lint from my navel, Linnit, a mother can't even be sure of that anymore, because, *tiens, mon amour*, I even heard of a debutante knock-up case where the boy who had to accept the onus of parenthood was one who had addressed himself to the fore, his buddy's lawyer got him to admit that cardinal fact by the following examination, 'Would you, Son, be so filthy and so foul as to address yourself to a young lady's dirt track.' 'Of course I wouldn't,' said this idiot called Son, 'do you think I'm a pervert?' 'Well, my client is, would, and did,' said the lawyer, 'so you are the proud papa, the Brains rest,' end of case.

"Take the undertaker out of it," said Linnit, "that's what disturbs your sense of peers and social compeers. A mortician is at a social disadvantage in stable structurification of society, but it's not to be calibrated on a final scale. If Tex Hyde were the son of a normal occupation father, for instance if Gottfried Hyde Senior was straight corporation exec like Rusty."

"No, no, no, Rottenbug, you're thinking like a tick again."

"If the boys were the same in the back room, so to speak, *sotto voce*," said Lenin Fink, "in the easy come and go, the rhodomontade—if you permit me—of similar breedings and backings, would you then object to the highly cathected vectors of their friendship?"

"Bless you, but I would."

"Tell me why, pie."

"Because Tex grew up a undertaker's son, fool! plunging his hands into dead people's vitals, picking up through his fingertips all sorts of black occult steamy little grimes of things, swamp music and black lightning and soundless thunder —purple wonders, it's like sleeping the night in a rotten old stump—who knows what song the maggots sing, and what aromatic intuitions inflame the brain. Herbs are the nerve to a fearsome underworld—listen, baby, I didn't get fucked by Aleister Crowley for nothing, those passes at the Black Masses," said Hallie, putting a gloved finger up to her dear chin—she is incidentally now lying her ass off because she's too young to know Aleister Crowley, but she's like her son, D.J., she's got to brag, better believe it.

Well, this has gone on long enough. Cause you ought to know who had produced this material. Color it rainbow. This has been D.J. presenting to you the private scene of his mother being psychoanalyzed by that clammy little fink, and if the illusion has been conveyed that my mother, D.J.'s own mother, talks the way you got it here, well little readster, you're sick in your own drool, because my mother is a Southern lady, she's as elegant as an oyster with powder on its ass, she don't talk that way, she just thinks that way. Do we understand each other now, son? You've had fun long enough. The serious shit soon starts. You're contending with a genius, D.J. is his name, only American alive who could outtalk Cassius Clay, that's lip, duck the blip, Orlando, it's right on your radar screen.

INTRO BEEP 2

The fact of the matter is that you're up tight with a mystery, me, and this mystery can't be solved because I'm the center of it and I don't comprehend, not necessarily, I could be traducing myself. Por ejemplo, the simple would state that Intro Beep One is a stream-of-conch written by me, and consequently commented upon by my mother up tight with her libido-drained psychoanalyst. But now you know Chap One with Fink Razzbah (rhymes with Casbah) is made up by me, D.J., alias Ranald such-and-such such-and-such Jethroe, Disc Jockey to the world (my mental connections are faster than anything afoot) and lightning which is a special case of light—how about that, Zack! is not proof against the rapidity of my investigations. For light is the content of a medium called lightning—Old Mc-Luhan's going to be breaking his fingernails all over again when he hears this. So watch out for D.J., muzz-fuckers. Gather here, footlings and specialists, hot shit artists, those who give head, and general drug addicts of the world, which means all you Hindus and professional football asshole buffs, and glom onto the confusion of my brain. It might be a tape recording, right? A tape recording of my brain in the deep of its mysterious unwindings. Maybe there will be a day when they discover how to dig it out, and then I will be the first living archaeological ex-humation, the first documentary source of prime existence, Living Man, here he thinks, listen in, Humphrey! and then D.J. will be revered because documentaries are the bleeding-heart gods of the future out there in old electronic land. Did you ever know the seat of electricity? It's the asshole. But what then is the asshole of elec-tricity? Why Creation, Catherine, that's what it is. I mean just think of the good Lord, Amen, and all the while we're sleeping and talking and eating and walking and pissing and fucking, excuse me, Lord, Amen! Amen! why, there's that

Lord, slipping right into us, making an *operation*
in the bowels of Creation so there's a tiny little
transistorized tape recorder not as big as a bat's
gnat's nut, why a million angels can dance on
the idiot pinhead of that tape recorder, DNA,
RNA, right? and it takes it all down, it makes
all the mountainous files of the FBI look like
paper cuttings in a cat-shit box, and so there is
the good Lord, king of the Rat Finks, I mean,
Sultan of the Wrathful Things, forgive me, Lord,
yeah, yeah, there *He* is getting a total tape record
of each last one of us, wow, double wow, rumble
woof, beat the tweeter, Vera Elvira, everything
you ever thought and your accompanying systole
and diastole and pisshole and golden asshole all
recorded, your divine intuitions and cloacal glut,
all being put down FOREVER on a tiny piece of
microfilm (or some such membraneous receptor)
all of it being compressed by the Super File
Compressor until the Lord wants to tune in on
you and so presumes to press a Nuraloid button
and all of you is transmogrified into one little
beep the microfilm gives up, cause that's it with
sound, infinitely compressible—with smell you
can waft your ass and nose from here to the black
hole of Calcutta—but every sound in a symphony
is contained in the bong of one gong, just as all
Creation is heard and felt in the shriek of the

tight wire in one pebble piss-or-pinch orgasm—
weep for all of us poltroons who have felt such
woe, Broad Lightning!—and now face your consequence, the Lord hears your beep, the total of
all of you, good and bad, sharp and flat, chords,
disharmonies and minor twelfths—wheeze! Give
up the breath—one of his angels passes you on.
To here or to there. Yeah.

Unless you can put false material into the tape
recorder. Think of that.

It opens this hypothesis. I, Ranald, S-and-S
Jethroe, working as D.J., may be trying to trick
Number One Above, maybe I'm putting false
material into *this* tape recorder, or jamming it—
contemplate! Maybe I'm making cheerful humor-
ous recs, belly laughter shit pressings when in
fact I'm sheer fucked right out of my mind, how
about that? Maybe all this humor here is absolute pretense, maybe—up your buns, J.D. Salinger
—I'm coming on like Holden Caulfield when I'm
really Doctor Jekyll with balls. I mean I got a
horror in me, honey, I will not tell you yet. I
will merely offer the clue—we have no material
physical site or locus for this record, because I
can be in the act of writing it, recording it
slipping it (all unwitting to myself) into the
transistorized electronic aisles and microfilm of
the electronic Lord (who, if he is located in the

asshole, must be Satan) or I can be expiring
consciousness, I can be unwinding and unravel-
ings of a nervous constellation just now executed,
killed, severed or stopped, maybe even stunned,
you thunders, Herman Melville go hump Moby
and wash his Dick.

Or maybe I'm a Spade and writing like a
Shade. For every Spade is the Shade of the White
Man, and when we die we enter their mind, we
are part of the Shade. And when Spades die?—
well, that depends on how you dig Niggers you
white ass chiggers says D.J. Come on now, says
D.J., what if I'm not the white George Hamilton
rich dear son of Dallas, Texas, and Hallelujah
ass but am instead black as your hole after you
eat licorice and chew black cherries, what then,
what if I'm some genius brain up in Harlem pre-
tending to write a white man's fink fuck book in
revenge, ever see an old black man roll his eyes
on a country road while some ice-green-eye redneck look him in and out saying what black
thoughts you have Sambo ass, and Mr. Black he
looking back and he see Whitey the Green Eye
from Texas with his ears moving in circles like
old wasp wings, zzz, and his sharp Scotch-Irish
White White White Man's Nose red as lobster
is a-hovering and a-plunging like a Claw, man,
look at the white-green snots way up high, Nig-

german, this is D.J. broadcasting from Texas, maybe, Doctor Jek out on his frants again, sick with the tick, ex-acid is my head, Love iS Death, HelL iS Death, it's square to be frantic, so bring in the cool, bring in the cool, D.J., tell the folk in the cool of the evening that they are listening to Mr. Big, Mister Big Blood, oh blood how rot is thy sting? So you can't know if I'm true-blue W??p-ass Texas even if I know and that's a fact, cause I know I'd like to walk up to Jesus some day and shake 'is hand and look 'em in the eye, and say Son, Y'may have lost the law suit, but have no hard feelings and come around again soon—we miss Y' down in this neck of the woods which ain't got much woods, nor trees for that matter, jus mud and dust and cattle and cow shit in abunnance, but Y're welcome, Y're surely welcome, Y're a man's man, Y're a peach, Y're a peach of a little whining Jew bastard, Jesus, each time I go hunting my wife won't fuck. That's Christianity for you—jes insists on using shit for axle grease in the heat of the chase.

Nonetheless, if you are really reading this and I am really writing it (which I don't know—it's a wise man who knows *he* is the one who is doing the writer's writing—we are all after all agents of Satan and the Lord, cause otherwise how explain the phenomenological extremities of hot shit and hurricane) but assuming howsomever that this huge metaphysical appropriation of the possibilities is valid that to wit that I, Dr. Jekyll, D.J. for genius, eighteen plus years old, is in fact writing this, then I better stop bullshitting the record and commit a few facts. Get set for my father in Chap Two. Release your horny masturbating hand. Engorge your lip. Take a fearsome trip.

★

CHAP TWO

★

D.J.'s father, the cream of corporation corporateness, Rutherford David Jethroe Jellicoe Jethroe, came back to Dallas after spending twelve years off and on moving around the world for Central Consolidated Chemical and Plastic, CCCP being what the boys called it till they found out the Red-ass Russians had their Communist Party initials CCCP, so they changed the name—look into the difficulties—an approval vote of the stockholders 1,178,008 to 241,642, change of listing on the stock market, reams of pure shit, reprinting of stationery, invoices, packages, loading, relettering boxcars—they a bunch of tight assholes running the inner mills of the mills, so guess the new name, you know it, they called it Central Consolidated *Combined* Chemical and Plastic, the new coagulation of title now being CCCCP or as the team began to say, 4C and P, which is an unhappy conjunction since how much can you foresee before you got—well, they say people in the Corporate life shoot their urine straighter than a '03 Springfield, we ain't Wasp-like for nothing, y' hear Rangoon? So back came Rusty after twelve big years in the foreign ass vineyards setting up operations for Double CC and Plastic, as *he* called it, his other fond name being Central Consolidated, cause they call it that too out where the reindeer run and the flying fishes try out their flying CIA fucks past Mandalay, and he was brought back in to head a new division for Four C-ing the cancer market—big lung subsidiary. Whereas Foreseeing Plastic wanted to get in on the bright new fortunes being made along the rim-scab of Carcinoma Cruds and Craters which D.J. is here to tell you is America's Last Frontier and Marching Estate, so leave Corporate Wisdom to its devices, they come up with a plastic filter for cigarettes which offers more pores in it than Sponge Valley, in fact if you perspire too much you can tape one of these cigarette filters to your armpit, that'll absorb the

Chinese cooking and general underarm funk;
should a petting party hose-down and gism-shoot
occur, as it may with the best of young friends
and associates, why, stick our plastic filter up
said girl's tootle and all misdirected gism will be
absorbed, no prononzo necessary here, but never,
unless you're the Earl of Roderick, try to proc-
tate it up her ass or she will never again be able
to tinkle and will die *emmerdé!!* Whang! Whang!
this plastic filter—trade name Pure Pores—is the
most absorptive substance devised ever in a vat
—traps all the nicotine, sucks up every bit of
your spit. Pure Pores also causes cancer of the
lip but the surveys are inconclusive, and besides,
fuck you!

Well, back came Rusty to Dallas to head Pew
Rapports—the filter with the purest porosity of
purpose—and Rusty was a heroic-looking figure
of a Texan, 6½, 194, red-brown lean keen of color,
eyes gray-green-yellow-brown which is approved
executive moderate shit hue color for eyes if you
want to study corporation norms mores and
tempos of shift and success in massive organi-
zational configurations, and since he was big
exec, what do you think he look and talk like?
Well, Clara, go to the rear of the line, he look
like a high-breed crossing between Dwight D.
Eisenhower and Henry Cabot Lodge, what the

buns do you think a corporation exec is going to
look like if he got the time to make his face grow
the way he want it to grow during all the Fifties
while he's overseas, I mean what face did he ever
see more of than Dwight D., and Henry C. working his axe, at the UN, these corporation eggzex
are full of will, man, they're strong as bulls these
hide-ass Waspy mules with their silvy rim specs,
I mean they go direction they want to go, their
hair too curly they go bald, their nose too long,
they sniff it up, their lips too fat, forget it, we're
talking about the wrong man, they tie that nice
dry-oiled West Point ramrod to their back just
like they're a tomato plant on a stick, I mean
they grow into a bat's ass if it help our astronauts along, Rusty and his ilk is hard-working.
He zip that corporation fly, dig, while working
as executive, and/or director, and/or special ad-
viser and/or consultant and/or troubleshooter
and/or organizer and/or associate of, and/or paid
employee for the 4C and P, the CIA, the C of C,
the FBI, the ADA (yeah, he gives contribs there
too right under the table—Rusty Jethroe and
Letterhead America are Up Tight) the Police-
men's Benevolent Society, the John Birch, natch,
the Dallas Citizens Council for Infighting and
Inflicting Symphonic Music, the Benevolent Order of Oilwell Riggers Drillers and Roughnecks,

the Warren Commission Boosters, the President's
Thousand Dollar Club, the Gridiron Club, the
UIA and 4A of D, that is the Underwriters, In-
surance Agents and Actuarial Agents Associa-
tion of America and Dallas, the NYSE (that's
Stock Exchange, Skeezix) the Anti-Defamation
League of the B'nai Brith, a passing honor they
gave him, totally honorary, believe you, the
RELM Cons—the Rotary, Elks, Lambs, Masons
Consolidated for corporation studs who jes ain't
got the time to spread out so they put it all in
one dead fuck building—and the Republican
Party, not to mention the Second Congregated
Anglo Episcopal and Conjoint Presbyterian
Clutch and Methodist Church of Maltby Ave-
nue, Dallas (that's St. Martin's, you faggot!) and
the Gourmet Wine and Pâté Plate and Fork
Society. Forget the country clubs unless you like
to read lists, the Dallas Elm and Tree Club, the
Dallas Cowboy Turtle Creek Cheering and
Chowder, TCU Boosters, SMU Boosters, the
Gala Ring and Ranch, Eddie Bonetti's Country
Club, take it from D.J., forget this shit. If Rusty
was to run around all year, which he does, he
still couldn't get his dick in every door for which
he's got a card, you know, even Diners' Club,
Carte Blanche, American Express, Rusty's a pig!
he's a real pig, man! It was all that dried-out

sunbaked smoked jerkin of meat his cowboy
fore-ass bears used to eat, I mean, man, they
used to use that hide for everything before they'd
eat it, they'd swab out their mare's dock with it,
wipe their own ass with it, pick up the pus from
the corner of their eye, blow their nose, mop the
piss off their boots, even use that dry old piece
of meat to wrap around their dick for stuffing
when they want to sodomize a real big fat slack
cow, why they repaired holes in their chaps with
it, they used to have to beat it with a hoe handle
before they could even cook it and fry it in axle
grease. I mean, man they were kind of tough. No
Frenchy Montesquious them. Crazy as wolves.
All greeneyed pricks. So, no wonder Rusty's a
pig. His cells are filled with the biological in-
heritance and trait transmissions of his ancestors,
all such rawhide, cactus hearts, eagle eggs, and
coyote. Now, Rusty rolls that Château Lafite-
Mouton-Rothschild around his liver loving lips,
and he can tell 49 from 53 from 59, all the while
thinking of 69. He sings the song of the swine,
D.J.'s daddy, nice fellow actually. Also forgot to
mention he's an unlisted agent for Luce Publi-
cations, American Airlines Overseas Division, and
the IIR—the Institute for International Research
—shit!, Spy Heaven they ought to call it.

Eh bien, you may now inquire, be you reader,

Good Lord, or the angel who's passing on this
message from my asshole transistor to God, why-
for does Doctor Jekyll have such a total rejec-
tion of all the positive elements in his rich secure
successful environmental scene including social
backing, strong sentiment, national roots, loci of
power, happy physical endowment (wait till you
hear more about that) and clearly individualistic
and highly articulated parents?

And D.J. says in answer: ever read *The Concept of Dread* by Fyodor Kierkegaard? No, well
neither has D.J. but now he wants to know how
many of you assholes even knew, forgive me,
Good Lord, that Fyodor Kierkegaard has a real
name, *Sören* Kierkegaard. Contemplate *that*. You
ass.

Anyway, D.J. is up tight with the concept of
dread. He don't have to read S.K. S.K. can stick
dread up his own ass. The time is near, man. D.J.
has ideas like nobody else. He sees through to the
stinking roots of things, contemplate Eternity
the poets might say, take a mind picture, D.J.
can watch his own ass being created on Time
Recaptured TV Time, eye on Big Daddy's back
while he stinging D.J.'s ma, D.J. a #1 ghost on
the #1 spermatozoa. Think of that. Maybe that's
how Herr Dread gets in. Cause D.J. has seen his
father while D.J. up high on pot, and face of

Rusty goes thru chord changes then. Strange sounds, man. Neo-occult chromatics. Crowns and diadems. An octave of farts. Hurtlings, hard-edge work, cockroach scamperings, caterwaulings, rivers of cream—oh, Mary, forget it, D.J. is putting you on, that's LSD shit and William Burroughs in horse land, not sweet old tea. No, via grass, man, D.J. has seen Rusty as follows: (1) the smiling Ike grin goes away, and so do all those Henry Cabot Lodge grins, instead there's a thin lippy old hole cut for his mouth—like the first slit on an operation—skin peels back, and in the wound there's teeth—D.J. happens to know those teeth are real, cause his daddy bit him once five years ago—that's a tale! (Can you wait for your next Intro Beep?)—but those teeth look like ten grand worth of superaesthetic dentures. And his nose takes a metamorphosis or two out of the Onassis Aristotle Bank of Ideal Forms. Well, now Rusty's got normally some kind of big pointy nose with fleshy backing, good shape, but it's a tool, man. On pot, it looks suddenly like a hand, got a red mean finger at the tip, stab you right in the middle of your lie, or grab your mouth and twist it off. It's a shit converter of a nose—any flunky talking to Rusty and not knowing what to say cause he's hiding some fuckup is going to find all that hardpan constipated

Texas clay in his flunky gut turning abruptly to
sulfur water and steam. Not to mention specks
of zipping around deepsea shit. Of course, if the
flunky farts in his panic, forget it, Rusty can't
bear the sight of a man who ever broke under
pressure. But it's Rusty's eyes kick off the old
concept of dread in D.J. Fyodor Sören Kierkegaard Jethroe because they remind him of his
favorite theory which is that America is run by
a mysterious hidden mastermind, a secret creature
who's got a plastic asshole intalled in his brain
whereby he can shit out all his corporate man-
agement of thoughts. I mean that's what you get
when you look into Rusty's eyes. You get voids,
man, and gleams of yellow fire—the woods is
burning somewhere in his gray matter—and then
there's marble aisles, better believe it, fifty thousand fucking miles of marble floor down those
eyes, and you got to walk over that to get to The
Man, which is only the way his eyes look to D.J.
when on pot, cause you know in a photograph
or just shaking his hand, Rusty's eyes are okay,
sort of dead ass and dull with a friendly twinkle
—typical American eyes—and when he's turned
on, like when he's ready to prong a passing cunt
in a hurry—which D.J. estimates is six eight times
a year—or when he's about to consummate the
big signing (listen to the silent bagpipes) in some

ten-month pass-the-buck or stand-and-fuck game
of negotiations, why then Rusty's eyes are like
yellow coals, liquid yellow fire ready to explode
in its own success. Horses away! Polo mallets up,
Bostwick! if D.J. wouldn't take to pot at family
dinners he might not have such a Fyodor Kierk
kind of dread looking into Big Daddy's chasm
and tomb. But that dread's out there, man. Because Rusty is also the highest grade of asshole
made in America and so suggests D.J.'s future:
success will stimulate you to suffocate! Yeah, if
they any higher grade asshole in America than
Rusty why they got something on the ball com-
parable to life stuff, cosmological matter, Zen
archery, hot shit satori, Highways and Byways
of LSD, or plain hardpan thriftily won, modestly
assumed, holy acquired plain old Christian Grace
and Get-up, Go, Spunk. Now, they ain't that
many in America. D.J. despite time overseas will
not presume to assert authority in these matters
for foreign lands, but in America the most stable
and dependable human product we turn out, and
our schools, businesses, armed forces, and legis-
lative halls are proud to be so filled with the
product, is a medium- to high-grade asshole like
Rusty, who in turn obeys the orders only of
G.P.A.—who, in case you forget, is Mr. Great
Plastic Asshole. So don't be too hard on Rusty.

He's a pig with a wild snouty mouth, but he's got good blood.

Okey-doke, Henry. The thing to understand is that a high-grade asshole is characterized by a specific and even unique property which endows him because of it with his rank—it is that a high grade of A.H. is not easily recognized as any kind of A.H., and usually appears the contrary. Despite the cock and bunghole details D.J. has furnished you up to here on some few of Rusty's opinions and habits, the portrait has been highly unfair to high-grade assholes because it has emphasized the hole rather than the high grade. Therefore, attention America to how Rusty shapes up in a contest against a man who is not an asshole—to wit, Mr. Luke Fellinka, head guide and hunter extraordinaire for the Moe Henry and Obungekat Safari Group on a hunting trip up in Brooks Range, north of Arctic Circle, Alaska. Yeah, follow along on this. Get your head clear. Get ready. Followers of D.J. are going to be hung on Alaska for a lot of high-grade genius rating consciousness now, because Rusty is the most competitive prick there is, and Big Luke is a sweet old bastard, who's so tough that old grizzly bears come up and kiss his ass. Yeah.

INTRO BEEP 3

Yeah, Rusty's a competitive prick, you know, he played for TCU, third All-American AP 1936, 1937, like back in there! look it up! and he was showing D.J. something few years ago on the back lawn of the Dallas ass mansion we inhabit, father and son—details on request, pen pal!—and he demonstrated to me I could not run around him. Well, of course D.J. did just that for a while, he ran the fucking ass off and around Rusty cause D.J. at thirteen had a presumptive hip dip halfback's butt about as big as Scarlett O'Hara's waist and he could use it like a double pin universal swivel, and Rusty had acquired a

considerable amount of dead ass sticking his
brave plunger up all blindly into the cunt-refined
wickedness of Hallelujah's sophisticated rumps
and vaginal radar rays masers and lasers. I mean,
he was like the charge of the Light Brigade, not
so light, and she was one with all those houris
and Fakirs and Cossacks and Turks up in the
hills who wait to pick each zippy point of meat-
nip and therefore know where to cut down on
the Light Brigade and cut off a piece of that
charge for themselves. O Kuklos, great god of
the seasons, bring back the fox trot, cause D.J.'s
embarrassed to tell what's next, how, he, thirteen-
year-old swivel ass flunkout in classics at the
time, was running Third Team All-America TCU
tackle Rusty Deathrow's middle-aged dead ass
into the Dallas lawn fertilizer when D.J. made a
fatal misestimate of reckoning—he felt sorry for
his dad. He let him tackle him just once. Jes
once—right in the dry linty Dallas old navel of
Texas. Rusty was so het up, he *flung* D.J. and—
mail in your protests—he bit him in the ass, right
through his pants, that's how insane he was with
frustration, that's how much red blood was in *his*
neck, and man, he hung on, he nearly lifted D.J.
up in the air with his deathly teeth—he would
have if he hadn't been a deacon at St. Martin's.
That poor D.J. He was a one-cheek swivel ass

running on one leg for the next ten minutes while Rusty tackled him whoong! whoong! over and over again. Trails of glory came out of his head each time he got hit. "Randy," said Rusty, afterward, "you got to be a nut about competition. That's the way. You got to be so dominated by a desire to win that if you was to squat down on the line and there facing you was Jesus Christ, you would just tip your head once and say, 'J.C., I have to give you fair warning that I'm here to do my best to go right through your hole.'" Actually, if Rusty had ever seen J.C. on the line he'd have shit, he'd have said with a little funky wink, "Are we going to be so fortunate as to get you for the Contemporary Speaker's Series at Southern Methodist?" no, D.J.'s here to say that Rusty bit his ass so bad because he was too chicken to bite Hallelujah's beautiful butt—she'd have made him pay a half million dollars for each separate hole in her marble palace. D.J., as you may have divined, is a manly clean-featured version in formal features of his mother, and don't look like a puma or a George Hamilton at all, light brown hair, green eyes, he's just good-looking, that's all. And he was a son of sufficiently decent comportment to follow his daddy's advice. So soon as the fucking game was over (can you imagine the two of them on the back lawn of that Dallas manse?) why D.J. just limped broke-ass to the gardener's shed, picked up a pick-axe handle, and bopped his daddy over the dead center of his head, blood still running down from that bite. When Rusty didn't fall and in fact an electric shock traveled from his head down the pick-axe handle into D.J.'s overheated heart, why our boy knew in some competitions sanity was better than being a nut, so he split, man, he took off on one leg and a wound in cheek of his ass, and it took a week of negotiations by his ma to bring him out of the hideout in Mineral Wells where she'd stashed him and into audience with his father again. Who, of course, sent him to military school out in the general vicinity of McQueeney, Texas. "If it was good enough for Pres. Eisenhower, it's good enough for you," well, that was a comic book military school, all Nazi-type Texas-style state trooper wolf bugger faggots and little languid queer types from Norlins. There was even a Frenchy Montesquiou. En passant, D.J. tied a couple of pricks into pretzels and made his escape, and could if so choosing have given Linnit Fixit material for his unwritten book on the grope habits of the Southwest.

Now, of course, Rusty Jethroe ain't an habitual asshole with anyone but his son. In fact, it was

an excess of love which produced such a high
focus and over the threshold area of hate as those
cuspy little marks on D.J.'s one of two buns
which D.J. now incidentally explains to those
Dallas debutantes and just plain common fucks
who are lucky enough to get drilled by him and
Tex, as the circular cornada produced by the
slivers of a horn shattered on a fighting bull
which he had engaged in a tienta south of
Guadalajara, Mexico, and what's the pity, he
tells the girls, is that he might have been able
to distinguish himself if it hadn't been for the
fact that the bull was hurt sufficiently to be with-
drawn from the fucking ring while they played
the Virgin of the Macaroon—that's how *dumb*
those young Texas cunts can be, better believe
it—and all the poor Mexican wetbacks sitting in
the stands threw cascades of hot piss at him
from their empty paper cups used originally for
beer (in one spout, out the other) and D.J. would
lick his lips, and look the sweet little Dallas cunt
in the eye, and say, "Honey, that piss smelled
just like your sweet little home-cooking crotch
before you get up in the morning to swab it
down," and your Disc Jockey here to tell that
would start a real fight in the back seat of the
car with D.J. his pants half-mast and laughing
his ass off, and the girl developing muscles like

cables made of guitar strings, they would have like to garrote him—the smell of her pussy is sacrosanct to a young girl! Mexican hot piss! Why even a little-headed, thin-nosed, big-jawed, six-foot Dallas girl would have imagination enough to know what Mexican hot piss would smell like from the Rio Grande all the way to the floodlands of Anchorage, Alaska. Or even beyond to the hunting cabin.

Thus, D.J. your hot hustling guide has by native wit brought you back to the confrontation between Rusty and Big Luke the Paragon Fellinka and Ollie Totem Head Water Beaver, and their guide assistants, and the various minions and flunkies and Tex and D.J. Nose to nose soon will be Luke and Rusty. Hold on.

CHAP THREE

Now Rusty was supposed to go originally on Alaska safari with his opposite number Al Percy Cunningham, the managing director of Tendonex, which is 4C and P's answer to Fiberglas. Rusty and Al Percy C. had reserved an Alaska guide eighteen months in advance, you know the type that is a guide for Charley Wilson or Roger Blough or J. Edgar—I mean, that's who you got to be if you want to get this guide right away, like he wouldn't even take Senators, and you was a Congressman and you wanted Big Luke Fellinka and his assistant Ollie the Indian Water Beaver, forget it, you could lie down on your

back and say Big Luke if you consent to be my
guide you or Ollie can take one big crap in my
mouth just for openers, and Big Luke would
yawn. D.J. and Tex read right away the #1 reason all the minions of the Great Plastic Asshole
were slobbering over the bear grease on Big
Luke's boots. It wasn't just because among Alaska
guides he was primus inter pares (you have just
had the first and last of D.J.'s Latin) it wasn't
cause he got eight clients out of the Brooks
Mountains once in a record September blizzard,
or fought a grizzly or two bare hand to a kind
of draw and had the scars to show it (looked
like vines and thorns had grown over an old seam
of welding on his back) it wasn't even his rifle
work which in offhand shooting could put in 25
one-inch five-shot clusters at 100 yards, and at
two hundred yards in a half-ass clearing of woods
could now and then drop a bullet into the eye
of an Alaska wolf as directly as you could drop
your finger in your own eye—no, what made Big
Luke The Man was that he was like the President of General Motors or General Electric, pick
one, I don't give a fuck, he had like the same
bottom, man, I mean D.J.'s here to tell you that
if you even a high-grade asshole and had naught
but a smidgeon of flunky in you it would still
start—you may purchase this in full confidence—

it would still start in Big Luke's presence to blow
sulfur water, steam, and specks of hopeless diar-
rhetic matter in your runny little gut, cause he
was a *man!* You could hang him, and he'd weigh
just as much as Charley Wilson or Robert Bone-
head McNamara, I mean you'd get the same intensity of death ray off his dying as you'd get
from some fucking Arab sheik who had ten thousand howlers on horses to whoop and scream
for the holy hot hour of his departure to Allah.
So you can see what a hoedown of a hunting trip
it would have been if Al Percy C. alias Kid
Tendonex and Rusty had each been burning up
that Alaska Brooks Mountain Range brush trying
to light a light of love in Big Luke's eye, but Al
Percy Cunningham was called off at the last by
the Astronaut Program hotline into 4C and P
because the real hoedown just that week of departure was between Fiberglas and Tendonex
to see who was going to get the contract to put
a plastic Univar valve and plug into the bottom
of the collapsible built-in space suit chemical
toilet in the Gemini (Roman Numeral Unstated)
which contract is no superhuge kettle of lobster
shit in volume dollars, but just a reasonable 58
million, although Tex and D.J. agree that little
Univar plug is First Priority, cause let it mal-
function and those astronauts will be swimming

in orbits of dehydrated processed food shit (their own—a gritty performance, eh Maurice?). However, it's edge. Does 4C and P, Tendonex Division, or FCA (Fiberglas Corp. of America) get to be the first to fling their product into space; besides there's rumors, Rusty tells us, that smooth plastic in outer space tends to exhibit Independent, Autonomous, Non-pattern-directed Ductile-type Magnification and Expansion Assertions in Non-Operational Gravitational Ultra-Multi-Mach Ellipsoid Program-Oriented Satellite Capsule Negotiations, which is to say that smooth plastic is growing plastic hairs on its palm while in such jerk off orbit. A big sweat is on. Whose research program has anticipated any of this? "Cunny's sweating this week," Rusty tells the boys. "I told him to load up with Pure Pores once his balls started to get wet, and he just gave me a sick little hunky hunk heh-heh. Probably wanted to haul off and split your dad with an axe."

But Rusty, au fond, is deeply in disappointment, not cause A. P. Cunningham ain't with him, but because the hunting trip is now downgraded. D.J.'s here to tell you that in secret Rusty feels like a movie star who's going out to pump for a weekend with the best new Pumper-head Penis in Cinemaville, and then hears she's missing the opportunity to have a commissary lunch with

Prince Philip or Baldy Khrushchev, before Baldy was an ex. Well, you know a movie star, she'd rather have Big K stomp his big shoe jes once in the crack of her ass while he's still Mr. Big than have her cunt stick-tickled into heaven for three days with no one up there in the redwoods to see except those guests invited to the exhibition like her mother, her father and her dramatic coach. "Hit high C next time you come, Chérie, we got to get through those vocal locks," says the dramatic coach.

Now D.J. suffers from one great American virtue, or maybe it's a disease or ocular dysfunction—D.J. sees right through shit. There's not a colon in captivity which manufactures a home product that is transparency proof to Dr. Jekyll's X-ray insight. He sees right into the claypots below the duodenum of his father, and any son does that is fit candidate for a maniac, right, T.S.? the point here, Eliot, is that D.J. will never know if Rusty dropped points in the early stages of his contest with Luke because he was dying inside for not being down at the Canaveral table where big power space decisions were being made by his opposite number, Wise-Ass Cunningham, or whether Rusty would have lost in the early stages to Big Luke on the best week he ever had, which is an ambiguity right at the center of D.J.'s message center. But proceed to study the scene.

Give Rusty his straight shot. If Big Al Percy Wise-Ass Cunningham had been there, the set of events would have had to be different. Take away A. P. Cun and what you got—ego status embroilments between numbers, guides and executives. All right—look into it. You may never get out.

First, Rusty spends no time trying to be the equal of Big Luke head on! He takes Luke's suggestions, is friendly but aloof. When Luke addresses him as Sir, Sir Rutherford Jet-Throne does not say call me Rusty. When Big Luke speaks to Rusty's two accompanying flunkies, Luke naturally picks them up by the handle of their first name, and Rusty, listening, chuckles like poor Clark Gable used to when he was near the end, that is indulgently and wisely, could be worse, man, cause the two flunkies—call them Medium Asshole Pete and Medium Asshole Bill —M.A. Pete (Asistant to Procurement Manager, Pure Pores Filters Company Office of 4C and P) and M.A. Bill (Personnel Director for Production Manager, Pure Pores et cetera Company Office of 4C and P) laugh each of them separately and respectively like Henry Fonda and Jimmy Stewart. Maybe it should be said that they are

Medium Assholes with a passing grade of C. Rusty could have done better, but kid you not, it ain't so easy. Talent ain't hanging on meathooks in corporation land, especially when you change plans and invitations at the last minute. Some Americans giving up a lot for the astronauts.

Now, with such for background on personnel, ask yourself Sherlock Onanist Holmes what were Rusty's expectations from this trip, I mean Rusty is corporation, right, that means he's a voice, man, he's a voice, got nothing unexpected ever to say, but he got to say it with quality. These corporation pricks are not there for nothing. They may be dumb and benighted, yeah, and D.J. has wasted his adolescence in their purlieus and company mansions and has eaten off their expense accounts all his days, D.J. knows them asshole to appetite, and can tell you, Horace, they are not all that dumb. Being medium-grade and high-grade asshole, they have high competence in tunnels and channels. They can all swim uphill through shit face first although in fact corporate faces are never seen to move, for they know enough not to try to read each other's corporate fish features when they can read each other's corporate ass voices. Man, they pick up what you're trying to slip by them, they buy nothing that's not tested, not voice-tested. So look at Rusty's problem. He goes on a Class A hunting trip—a Charley Wilson, John Glenn, Arnold Palmer, Gary Cooper kind of trip, next thing in top category you might say to a Jackie Kennedy Bobby Kennedy Ethel and the kids trip—Rusty's stepping up out of category, reaching just a bit, but if he makes out, if he comes back and is able to say, "Well, it was not a record honey-girzzly by any means, it didn't weigh out at more than twelve hundred, but Big Luke thought I got off a fair shot, and was, truth to tell, impressed with the coincidence that George Humphrey dropped one in the same glen just five years ago."

Now, pick up on the potential pitfalls. If Rusty is bird-turding he's got a lot of cabbage verbiage for which he can be faulted on. Take: fair shot. That could mean great shot; could mean piss-ass shot. George Humphrey's name equal to Pope Pius in certain executive Dallas ass chambers; therefore it's got to be dropped like a feather on velvet. Honey-grizzly has to be enunciated as if you was up tight enough with that variety of bear to tweak his nuts. So on. Mark this, fellow Americans, and file it 2R—Ready Reference— each time Rusty runs into mood-gearings of attention back home in the office, he is going to have to turn to M.A. Pete or M.A. Bill and say, "Isn't that so, Pete? isn't that so, Bill?" and they're going to have to say, "It sure is, Rusty," and say it without a trace of strain, they're yes-men, it is expected of them to be dauntless in their gut yes as they go through the yes ass gears, but perfection breeds perfection, the critical ear gets as sharp as a mad-dragster maniac-type genius listening to two 427 cubic inchers put in tandem—their yes has to have perfection precisioned. Well, even with professional bull-shit, and that's the secret of the corporation—it is filled with men who are professional bullshit packers—there is a limit. A yes-man will strain his gut to produce—they are the unsung heroes of America (reason they're unsung is they can't get their tongue out of the boss' ass long enough to sing) but strain a gut as they may they can-not strain it past its own true natural elasticity. Something bona fide has got to happen, they can't just go up to Alaska woods, get drunk for a week, buy a bear skin in Fairbanks or McGrath, take pictures, and slip a suppository up the folks back home, those Texas ears too sharp. There'd be a soupçon of caviar shit in the voice and that would put a rick-tick-tick in the narrator's disc. So Rusty's got to produce something big enough for his boys, M.A. 1 and M.A. 2, to say you're right, Rusty, with an easy harmonious concordium of voice, a choir of Texas ass-purring where the yeah boss you go right ahead and kick my Nigger ass gets a Texas hum. For then corporate power is cooking in Rusty's veins.

So Rusty's problem is simple. He can't begin to consider how to go back without a bear. He got a corporation mind. He don't believe in nature; he puts his trust and distrust in man. 5% trust, 295% distrust. He figures if Big Luke wants him to tag a bear, that's the ball game—if Big Luke don't want him to, then Rusty is left close to being a dead ass this season. He'll be caught stalking around in the brush with a guide who's holding such a rep he can afford to save himself for his major clients and make the minor executives like Rusty do a little work for him. Rusty has taken a full estimate of Big Luke and has this to decide: man to man, if you put each in the other's job from birth, Rusty could have done everything Luke did except those twenty-five five-shot one-inch offhand clusters, cause that ain't practice, that's magic, and Rusty is modest about magic, but Big Luke in Rusty's shoes would not have gone as far because he might be, bend your head (in secret) too fucking lazy. First thing, smack off, Luke tells Rusty that it's not the best season this year for bear, and when

Rusty, all modesty and politeness, allows as how he'd like to make a push against these poor possibilities, Big Luke, who's coming on one hundred out of one hundred relaxed, kind of smiles, crinkly introductory humor humoring, and says, "They're scarce now. When bear get lonesome they can smell far." Well, Big Luke got a presence, not much of a face, just a big sunburned mug of a face like a pie with a lot of scars in it, he looks just like Big Ollie Water Beaver except paler, for Big Ollie is as dark as an old leather jacket, but Big Luke sends out a wave every time he has a thought, you can feel it, and around him you can get messages back, you can feel that one bear out in those woods sending out its message—don't come near, motherfuck—that message transmitted from the bear to Big Luke and relayed to us, you can tune in on the madness in the air, you now know where a pine tree is rotting and festering somewhere out there, and red ants are having a war in its muck, and the bear is listening to those little ant screams and smelling that rotten old pine, and whoong goes his nose into the rot, and he bites and swallows red ants, slap, bap, pepper on his tongue, he picking up the bite of death in each ant and the taste of fruit in the pulp, digging that old rotten tree whose roots tell him where we are, capisce, Luigi? There's a fucking nervous system running through the earth and air of this whole State of Alaska, and the bear is tuned in, and Big Luke, and Ollie and the assistant guide packers, and the ants, and Tex and D.J., and the air, man, the air is the medium and the medium is the message, that Alaska air is real message—it says don't bullshit, buster. And Rusty of course reads this not, cause Big Luke is pouring salt in his ass. Big Luke is *mean.* "Lot of caribou," Big Luke says. "Think about starting the week with caribou." Well, Rusty would as soon start the week with rabbits as caribou deer. D.J. reads this easy—let Rusty presume to come back from the Brooks Mountain Range of Alaska to Big D, Texas, air distance 3,247 miles (check not on this detail, for D.J. has just estimated it—who the mother-butter is going to make such a small-ass measurement of distance but a hotel lobby type tourist?) let Rusty travel all that round trip 6,000 plus miles, spending 6,000 plus dollars on D.J. and himself —not all tax-deductible either, you fuck, and present himself at 4C and P with a deer's head and no bear. Rusty and his status (who are as up tight with each other as two plump yoni— that's Hindu for cunt, son!—doing sixty-nine in the long Hindu night) can now take a double pine box funeral—they'll never get off his ass at

Combined Consolidated, no, no, the office staff will wet their little pants waiting for Christmas so they can send him an anonymous set of antlers off some poor ass spavined Texas buck twice the antlers in width of measurement and holding four more points than the one he air-freighted back from Alaska—you know they'll do that at the office if they got to dig up an old ranch hand's bones and glue them together for antlers, Rusty knows a piss cutter when it scratches his scrotum—thank you very much, Mr. Luke Fellinka, but no thanks on that deer.

"Say, Luke," says Rusty, "I sure hope you put the hair on a bear for us cause I'm feeling like the poorest safari victim you've had all year," and Big Luke says, "We, sir, have no safari victims, just happy clients and disappointed clients, and sometimes you can't tell by looking at their face, not by the time they get home."

INTRO BEEP 4

This of something black-ass and terrible, black
as a tumor in your brain, black as the black-ass
consciousness of that crippled Harlem genius
which D.J. shoves up for gambit as one possible
embodiment for his remarkable brain. Shit, shit,
and shinola, death in your breath, death in your
breath gives a hump to the lung like the silent
sound of a pocket turning inside out in the
black-ass black-ball closet. Bishop Berkeley, goes
the mad comptometer in old D.J.'s head, am I
the ideational heat of a real crazy-ass broken-
legged Harlem Spade, and just think myself D.J.
white boy genius Texan in Alaska imagining

my opposite number in Harlem land, when in fact, Good Lord, when in fact, I, D.J., am trapped in a Harlem head which has gone so crazy that I think I sitting at a banquet in the Dallas ass white-ass manse remembering Alaska am in fact a figment of a Spade gone ape in the mind from outrageous frustrates wasting him and so now living in an imaginary white brain, or is that ether-load man? is not D.J. really white, really walking at sixteen into the vale where the death of breath crosses all eternal wires, and D.J. is merely tapped in for touches of intellectual luxury to some fucked-up little bedridden Spade, or is that the abortive consciousness of a tumor beginning right under the medulla oblongata of his white brain a knot of psychic hatreds congregated in molecule dance to design a new kind of flesh, sarcoma, melanoma, carcinom' and Nome and Barrow, Alaska, Fairbanks—late afternoon?

CHAP FOUR

Well, by the light of the twilight D.J. does a little estimating. There's guides and guides in Alaska, some for scratch-ass hunters, and some for poobahs where the idea is to bring the trophy to the man so that John Foster Dulles types can make the record book without ever getting their cheese wet crossing a brook. By the end of the first night in Fairbanks, while they lolling around getting acquainted in a super deluxe motel bar of a dark chocolate-red velvet interior looks like it was flown up from Seattle (which it was, en route from Hawaii where they imitating the English Pump Room in Threadnelly Gate, London W. 1) D.J. and Tex analyze it out—Big Luke used to be a big hunter, but those grizzly scratches have weakened his Arnold Toynbee coefficient— he interested less in challenge than response—if he caught his share of the three grand a head without having to lead various grades of assholes and tough but untrained adolescents into the brush to look for Mr. Wounded Honey Grizzly holding the head of a magnum in his bear gut and a last dream of murder in his bear eye, well, Big Luke, despite the big man death-guts cha- risma, may have had his day. Who's to say there is no actors in Alaska?

Listen to the dialogue: "Luke, I'm a stubborn Texas son of a bitch," says Rusty, lifting his bourbon in the Fairbanks, Alaska, motel bar (empty near but for three old couples from Kansas on an airline tour of Anchorage, Fair- banks, Barrow, Nome, and Juneau, with dips into Kotzebue, Unalakleet, and Homer, and a brother and sister at University of Alaska entertaining their ma and pa up to visit from Portland)—this lack of activity may be given total attributability to the vacation-directed personal vector impera- tives of the American mind which shuts up action after Labor Day. This is after Labor Day, early September in Alaska, two years (to remind you) before the period of D.J.'s consciousness running through his head, hence form is more narrative, memory being always more narrative than the tohu-bohu of the present, which is Old Testament Hebrew, cock-sucker, for chaos and void, "Yeah, I'm stubborn," sighs Rusty tenderly, sipping his bourbon like his mother had brought him up on mother's milk and moonshine, "I don't want to carry on about where I've hunted, because I could tell you about going for wild boar in Bavaria, and for elephant in Africa—although I never got the elephant, my gun-buddy Ram Federstone got it, I just got a kudu, a snake, an African antelope, and a zebra. I always say I paid five thousand—you count them—bucks for a goddam convict suit."

"How about that, Pete?" said M.A. Bill, getting in the big chuckle first.

"Shee-it, Rusty," said M.A. Pete, "that's a beautiful set of head and shoulder zebra stripes in the Bomb Shop," (which is what Rusty calls the Jethroe den, the Bomb Shop).

Rusty turns his head, like a maidenhead being told she's pretty, sort of a "It's not for me to say," and then he turns his keen shit hue executive eyes on Big Luke and says, "I even got in on a tiger hunt with the Maharajah of Pandrasore, but that I don't count because I was present in 'semiofficial function'," a big wink, man, whatever the fuck semiofficial function is CIA supposed to convey, professor, "and we didn't even carry rifles. There was an array of Hindu peons up ahead each with a kris on a bamboo stick, and they did the sticking. The Maharajah's function, it turns out, is to be some variety of the Great White Hunter. The majesty of his attendance on the hunt brings tigers up where there were none before. If there's a tiger this side of Tibet the Maharajah's magnetism will draw him. Sure as bird shit on a parasol, damn if we didn't attract three tigers."

"Maybe I get to learn a couple of new things about hunting from you," says Big Luke F.

"Say, Mr. Fellinka, I may look like a variety of Texas bull, but not that big, I swear. No, no, no. I'm not here to instruct, I'm here to imbibe. At the foot of a master. I just want to make a point, teacher. I want to cut the fiercest mustard you ever tasted with a piece of bear steak, I want to behold Bruin right in his pig red eye so I'll never have to be so scared again, not until I got to face The Big Man. Listen, Luke, here's what I suspect is true—it is that you are the Maharajah of this woods and this range of earth, and so I'm expecting you to make the impossible become directly possible and we're going to carry our stretch of hunting to what I would call a successful termination."

"Was a berry blight in August," says Big Luke, "Now the bear are out digging roots in the brush. That's a little thick there. A little too thick to bring a party in. Get a thorn in your eye, gun gets tangled, you can be looking at the ground about the time Friend Bear is putting an arm over your neck."

"Say, now," says Rusty, "this is a guaranteed bear trophy hunt, now isn't it?"

"Well, sir," says Big Luke's Tour Guide Coordinator, Mr. Kenneth Easterly, who has met the group at the airport, and brought them along Airport Way to the motel, name now forgotten, Alaska Cavalier maybe, or Fairbanks Frontier Arms, some such (Fairbanks being near as flat-ass a city as Dallas has naturally lots of humperdick in the names) "well, sir," says Kenneth E who's the olive oil in this operation, "you have a guaranteed bear trophy in the specifications of the safari contract—that's for shit-and-sure," says Easterly, cause people he's addressing are Texans; if they was New York Jew ass Banker sportsmen, he'd say "certified." Nods his head, as if he's shaking his hand, "Yes-sir, there's a rebate of five hundred per head if we neglect to get you in proper range for a shot at a visible grizzly, although I want to tell you, we've never had to rebate it."

"Everybody who's taken your safari has gotten Mr. Grizzer," asks Rusty, "or had a fair shot?"

"No, sir. Not everybody. Some few do not have that peculiar good fortune. But they don't want the rebate. After they see the way Big Luke and Big Ollie take them around through the Brooks Range—that's *wilderness*, Mr. Jethroe —way they cook for 'em, tote for 'em, skin and pack, they're feeling sufficiently good, they've had the kind of hunting experience the desire for which brought them out here in the first place."

Rusty just shakes his head. "I don't believe I follow you, *boy*."

"Mr. Jethroe," says Kenny E., "we have the best guide in Alaska, and the finest clientele. We're here to take you around and give you *proper* hunting. We're not in competition with the counters. There are counters out in that wilderness, hunters of medium income (and medium ability to stick the muzzles of their rifles into a muddy piece of ground) who have none-theless saved their pennies to come here—it's the experience of a lifetime for them, and as you know, sir, the experience of a lifetime excites *greed* in the common man and a terror of being cheated. So they are out to get everything they can. They count every last pelt, they'll twist the tape measuring a Dall's horn to get an extra quarter of an inch on the length of it, they'll use handload cartridges make you gasp—it's a wonder simple steel can stand it—they hunt from four in the morning to midnight before they get back to camp, up at four again, they bring out every last piece of meat they can tote, or they don't even cut themselves a steak, just take the head and leave the flesh, imagine! and they maim, Mr. Jethroe, they maim game all over the damn place and then let them suffer. We ain't like that. We have the finest people in America come to us, we wouldn't even know how to advertise—we just hope too many people don't hear about us or the simple fine standard of clientele we possess might be adulterated. Because we offer hunting which is reasonable, decent in its risk, fair to the game, and not utterly deprived of comfort. We do not consider it decadent to have a book or two in the bunkhouse, and if Big Luke knows how to make a mixed drink, well, whiskey sours sweeten the heart after a long day of hunting, I like to claim."

"That's A-OK," says Rusty, "but the bear is the integral part of this expedition."

"Yessir, it is," says Easterly, "provided the bear is in a reasonable state."

"The bear are bad now," says Big Luke.

"What do you mean bad?"

"Changing their habits," Big Luke says. It comes out. All the good news. It seems there's been too much hunting in the Brooks Range. That's the confession of Kenny Easterly. The Moe Henry and Obungekat Safari Group (which is the exclusive George Humphrey special they are on right now) is no longer so alone in bringing its fine people up into that Arctic Circle, all the counter-type safari groups like Hunting, Ltd., and the Sam Sting Safari are pouring in too. The wild game is changing its psychology.

Big Ollie speaks up—his first speech. He talks like a cannibal in a jungle bunny movie. "Brooks Range no wilderness now. Airplane go over the head, animal no wild no more, now crazy."

"Say, friends," says Rusty, "I didn't come to Alaska to debate the merits and vices of technological infiltration."

Big Luke presents the case: "In August, three grizzly been wounded by other safaris in our hunting range. They get told not to move in but they move in. They, like you, sir, thought I'm the one to call the tiger so they hunt near me. They wounded and they neglected to follow up, and they left us three very mean grizzly, right in our own hills and lands up there. Now consider. A mean grizzly has only to smell a man and he is half-crazy. He does not come forward half-nice, half-mean, to take his look, nor does he go the other way—he thinks of how to kill. He circles, he stays downwind from the hunter. He remembers the bullet, that bullet maybe tore his intestine, that is a terrible pain. A bear feeling such pain, sir, is in my opinion, struck as if by lightning and so picking up in certain ways the intelligence of man."

"I see," says Rusty, "you're going to keep us well up above timber so no bear can sneak near on us. We'll have to spend our week climbing rocks just to get a shot at five hundred yards down on some mountain goat across a canyon."

"I'll give the best hunting for conditions," says Luke.

"Let's specify," says Rusty.

A sad-ass show. It flickers off, on, off, for ninety minutes, a muted hot shit hurricane. Finally, Big Luke hints that Rusty can have his rebate now, his deposit, his contract and his week, and that is the end of the first contest, for if there is one thing worse than coming back with no bear, it is coming back a rejectee and rebatee from the Moe Henry and Obungekat Safari

Group. If they could satisfy Old General George
C. Marshall in his hunting days, who is Sir Jet-
Throne to complain? Now he saves face. He
compromises, he agrees Luke will give the word
on when they go for grizzer. Say. They all go to
bed in rooms with a foam-rubber mattress, pink-
tile bathrooms, and Venetian blinds, and in the
morning, load gear and all ten men into three
Piper Apaches with amphibian floats and take
off for the Brooks Range where each plane
makes a tasty light water-slap of a landing in a
lake, Dolly Ding Bat Lake, where there's an
M.H.O.S.G. (for Moe Henry, et cetera) bunkhouse on the shore which is a pine forest so full
of boon in the smell it could make you a religious
nut, except D.J. does not dig pine resin out of
sight—he likes something a hint more funky if
he is entering concupiscent relations with the
penumbra of the Lord, ho, ho, but this bunkhouse which is a pâté foie of an Alaska bunkhouse is not theirs for long—they unload the
planes, then load up on packhorse, and work up
a trail all afternoon, a dog ass trail which gets
dull and then monotonous dull cause it's pine
forest and dwarf birch and not spectacular for
being up above the Arctic Circle, Rusty is com-
menting it's just as dull as all of Canada, and
then colors start to dim which gives a hint of

some kind of North, cause the rocks have a thin
gray, and the bark is gray on the trees and there's
a pinched look beginning to appear in the turf, a
mossy mean turf like dry bog crusts, the trees
get more individual, they have a continuing life
story now with the wind. Then timberline. Final
timberline, sharp and clean, a little park of grass.
They're up high on gray domes looking across
to other gray domes, and rising further until
even the fold of the canyon is dry of moss, and
the packhorses are hawking their breath, and
Big Luke finally picks on a shielded-in kind of
square saddle between some hunched-up bare
knolls, Big Luke calls it a basin, near to a black-
ass basin by the time they get there, and put up
the tents, Ollie makes the fire, et cetera, roast
beef hash with dehydrated pears, good by God!
on a white gasoline cookstove. D.J. and Tex ex-
hausted by the dialectic of the night before fall
out into dead-ass air mattress sleep with the
smell of the North on a September night, a tricky
clean smell, like a fine nerve washed in alcohol
and lightly powdered to get the rut of flesh off.

Next morning, on a light windless dawn, Tex
and D.J. get out of bed, start to brush their teeth
in a rill of a stream coming up out of a mountain
spring, that water presenting itself to the teeth
like sunlight on snow, and Tex saw, just then, a

wolf standing and pointing a half mile above
the timber, just standing there and studying the
dawn in a wolf silence like he had come to some
conclusion about the problems of life and occupation, near-relatives, in-laws, phratries, associates, herbs, roots, and grubs. Tex took him
down with a shot into the gut and at first he
could have been there dead, the animal fell and
for an instant the hills clapped together. Down
at timberline trees shifted, air moved in the wave
which follows a breaking of glass, and then the
wolf was up and running, but with a sick ass
lunge like a broken fly, and then slowed, stood
still, bore off at a bleeding ass walk back to the
woods, and Tex run after him and got him at
two hundred yards; one miss, one hit into the
back of the shoulder and the lungs. The look on
Big Luke's face was amiable like any boy who
could hit a wolf at four hundred yards was not
totally undeserving of guided service. Well, he
got down and gave us each a cup of blood to
drink and that was a taste of fish, odd enough,
and salt, near to oyster sauce and then the taste
of wild meat like an eye looking at you in the
center of a midnight fire, and D.J. was on with
the blood, he was half-sick having watched
what Tex had done, like his own girl had been
fucked in front of him and better, since he had

had private plans to show Tex what real shooting might be, and here was Tex, King Front Sight Indian Hunter, Killer of Wolves. D.J. next thing was on his hands and knees, looking into that upper Yukon wolf mouth, those big teeth curved like tusk, and put his nose up close to that mouth, and thought he was looking up the belly of a whale, D.J. was breathing wolf breath, the just dead air from the dead interior, but raucous breath, all the fatigue of the wolf running broken ass to the woods and the life running the other way from him, a crazy breath, wild ass odor, something rotten from the bottom of the barrel like the stink of that which is unloved, whelp shit smell, wild as wild garlic, bad, but going all the way right back into the guts of things, you could smell the anger in that wolf's heart (fucked again! I'll kill them!) burnt electric wire kind of anger like he'd lived to rip one piece of flesh from another piece, and was going to miss it now, going to miss going deep into that feeling of *release* when the flesh pulls loose from the flesh, and there D.J. was sweating, cause he was ready to get down and wrestle with the wolf, and get his teeth to its throat, his teeth had a glinty little ache where they could think to feel the cord of the jugular, it was all that blood he'd drunk, it was a black shit fuel, D.J.

was up tight with the essential animal insanity of things.

That, friends, was the beginning of the hunt. Not so bad. Big Ollie came up, asked Tex if he wanted the wolf for a trophy. Tex gave a blow of breath to his front sight. That's all the tension he was going to show. "I don't want no wolf for a trophy," he said. Ollie then studied the animal, nodded, suddenly dipped his finger in the blood, sucked it with a quick-popping sound of his cheek like a cook testing a cake batter, then took out a knife and cut the wolf's head off, one twisting cut of the knife for the vertebra at the neck, one long sawing swinging cut for the rest. Then he gave the head to the boys for a look. There were two eyes open on El Lobo, both yellow coals of light, but one eye was Signor Lupo, the crazy magician in the wolf, and his eye had the pain of the madman who knows there's a better world but he is excluded, and then the other eye, Willie Wolf, like a fox's eye, full of sunlight and peace, a harvest sun on late afternoon field, shit! it was just an animal eye like the glass they use for an eye in a trophy, no expression, hollow peace maybe, and Big Ollie dug a shallow pan of a hole with his knife in the crust bog tundra, whatever that dry shit moss was, and set the wolf's head in it, muzzle pointing to the north, and covered it over. Then he took a broken twig and laid it in a line with the end of the muzzle, but pointing further North, then got down on his hands and knees and touched his nose to the stick and said nothing for a moment.

"Always remember, boys," said Rusty, who had come up at the end to be part of our blood drinkers' breakfast group and coffeeclutch, "you don't get your proper paganism until you pay these dee-luxe prices."

"What he up to, Mr. J.?" said Tex.

"Well, you're looking at him, Indian to Indian, Tex, and don't forget ah got a drop of the fucking redskin elixir too, he's telling that wolf he respects him and not to spread the word, not to get grizzler turned on. I bet Ollie's telling him not to forget that when he was alive, he and Big Grizzler were not rushing to be asshole buddies, so please don't start a union now."

★

INTRO BEEP 5

★

That's it about a High-Grade A.H.—they can surprise you by times. D.J. is thus proud of his dad for filling Tex in that he could almost revise his opinion of Rusty if it wasn't for his Big Daddy's shit-licking propensity to have a chameleon pussy sphincter changeling of a voice—get Rusty out in the woods and he's Texas ass, man, common as dirt, hard as nails, he could crunch a clamshell with his asshole, rolls his prejudices around in his throat like a fat cricket in honey—but insert him behind a dinner table with candles, tablecloth, nubian black-ass Washington, D.C. type Pullman Porter butlers (Hallelujah actually has one working steady which leaves most of the North Dallas hostesses stricken into electrified shit, for, man, they got a scale for how rash and rough and poor white redneck raw yore lady's ass still is, and Hallelujah obviously got skin on her butt as sweet as the average plump dear woman has on her full sail of tits.) Yeah! Butter wouldn't melt in Hallelujah's butt, and you could think Rusty was buttering his bread in the same ingredient at a dinner table (where this reminiscence of hunting began sometime ago to run in narrative form) because, Repeat, all you deficient heads out there and nascent electronic gropers, memory is the seed of narrative, yeah, and D.J. grassed out at a formal dinner in his momma daddy's Dallas house with Tex in white smoking jacket across the table has brought back gobs of Alaska hunt memory two years before including the critical contrast in Rusty's voice between down home talk (biggest Texas ass accent in the corporation) and Cosmo high-fashion dinner talk, gentry ass style, no ideas, but a thousand fine names. Tonight they're entertaining the ex American Ambassador from Bringthatpore, shit! old lover of Halleloo's and various North Dallas matrons (street names on request) who got a Roman candle up their ass on what might come

up in Death-row Jethroe's southern manse this
eve. This is two years later, right now, but the
inside of the brain is always the present even if
it is memory two years old, and wolf blood drunk
that morning like wine is the up and Adam of
D.J.'s racing or expiring consciousness up now
right in the Brooks Mountain Range, and what
has happened after the wolf is that one of the
medium assholes, Pete, in fact, has just wounded
a caribou, right where they're all standing looking at Signor Lupo's old magician wolf grave,
and he has done it with a horror head of a gun
and cartridge, wait and hear, and everybody's
ass is now triple slung, cause they got to get up
from the wolf without breakfast and track that
wounded caribou. Poor Medium Asshole Pete.

CHAP FIVE

Well, now here, let's give a rundown on the guns for those good Americans who care. And those who don't, shit, they still get the chance to encounter a lot of meaningless names and numbers which they can then duly repeat at cocktail parties for new name grabbers.

Rusty, well now he's got, well you be sure Rusty is holding, in fact D.J. is now canny to save him for later. So here's Luke and Ollie. Luke got a Model 70 Winchester .375 Magnum restocked (with maple Japanese Shigui finish) and remodeled by Griffin & Howe with a Unertl 2½× scope, and that little rifle and cartridge could knock down anything but an elephant, and if the elephant had just gotten fucked, it would knock him down too. Luke don't need that gun, he could hit and take and flatten anything he wanted in Alaska with his second gun, old Swedish Husqvarna .30-06, restocked and remodeled, also Unertl 2½× scope (Luke was agent for Unertl for a while) which handles a 180-grain bullet on a very flat trajectory, a real 300–400 yard bap of an ice picker, extra high up over 3 thou in velocity delivered at the muzzle. Whereas Ollie has the same gun D.J. has, a factory-bought Remington 721, and both he and D.J. have worked the stock themselves. Ollie has all kinds of ivory totems and taboos inset in his grip and comb, including a profile of wolf head (hot shit and coincidence, Claudia!) and he got a nice Lyman Alaska 2½× scope. D.J. on his side has just done a little stupid ass inconclusive whittling into his Rem 721 stock—in truth it's a mess—forget it! Scope? He got a nice Stith Bear Cub 2½× scope with Stith mounts.

Tex has a factory-bought Winchester .270 Model 70 with a Weaver K-3 Tilden mount, neat as that. If he was a fink, D.J. would whisper that the first 400 yard shot which hit the wolf, considering it was done with a good .270 like the Winchester 70, was nothing truly spectacular,

for Tex had set his Weaver K-3 for 250 yards
the day before when they crossed timberline.
So, at 400 yards, even with a big 180-grain
bullet (and the corresponding big-ass load of
powder) he knew he wouldn't drop twenty
inches below the cross hair, never, at four hundred yards, so it wasn't that hard to put the dot
a bit above wolf's back and hit in eight inches
or ten inches below his spine. Anyway the whole
fucking kill was unaesthetic, cause a 180-grain
bullet which lets a wolf walk away after hitting
him must hit no closer than a red-hot poker
along his ass. Fact, that's what on examination
the first shot proved itself to be, for the weight
and hard nose of the bullet (bought to pene-
trate a grizzly hide) went right through the
wolf's two legs, breaking only one. Well this
fine critique ain't just piss grapes from D.J., because proof is that he is now repeating Tex
Hyde's very own critique of his own shot. "If I
hadn't been fever ass," says Tex, "I'd have taken
the time and got the 100-grain soft nose maga-
zine into Winnie, and I could have torn a hunk
of old Wolf right out of his heart so he didn't
have to suffer and we didn't have to chase. I can
hit *anything* with the hundred grain. That was
a fink and fuckup kill, D.J."

Which brings up Rusty, who travels like a

big-ass hunter. That Apache looked like it was
vomiting big equipment out of its guts, yeah, he
got for instance a .404 Jeffrey on a Mauser Magnum action with a Circassian walnut stock, one
love of a custom job by Biesen with Zeiss Zielklein 2½× on Griffin & Howe side mount for
Gun #1. Gun #2 is Model 70 Winchester rechambered to .300 Weatherly Magnum, Stith
Bear Cub scope, bird's-eye maple stock, et cetera,
et cetera. Gun #3 is Winslow Regimental Grade
7 mm. Remington Magnum with FN Supreme
400 action and Premium Grade Douglas barrel,
ivory and ebony inlays in the stock, basket
weave carving on both sides of the forearm and
pistol grip, Redfield Jr. mounts, Redfield 2×-7×
variable scope.

Gun #4 is Ruger . . .

Gun #5 . . .

Forget it. This account has now come right
down to the gnat in the navel of the whole week
of hunting which is Sweet Medium Sweet Asshole Pete who don't know about hunting enough
to go out and shoot at Texas cactus (which, if
you know how to plug it proper. dies with a
scream of Pulque blood gushering up and out
and an absolutely foul breakwind of Peyote gas)
no, Pete has grown up with a nice Savage 99
lever action .250 deer gun, and he runs and

freezes his own scared hot shit in a suburban rental frozen food locker when he gets the invitation to Alaska from Rusty, for that means a two- to five-year expediting of his dangerously dull slick as owl shit ascent of the corporation ladder provided he can make it on this Yukon expedition. So he runs out and he borrows a Savage 110 bolt action with Weaver K-4 scope from his deadly daddy (who years ago never thought enough of Pete's shooting to give him the 110, but laid, instead, the 99 lever action on him for Christmas). Well, that takes one nightmare out of Pete's head which is cocking that 99 fuck-your-finger lever while a grizzly, perfectly capable of eating whatever the Savage 99 .250 will throw, ambles and slides and tears across the brush at him. And it warms his heart cockles, cause it's the first treasured thing his daddy ever loaned him. (His daddy's beginning to breathe thin.) Well, Pete now starts hearing about the bolt action 110. It will stop any game, yeah, if the shot is *well placed*. Strangle that little news. Pete ain't looking to make a career of placing his supershots in superb array anywhere but in the office jungle. Don't tell him about 180-grain Core-Lokt or Silver Tipt, he wants a grenade and bullet all in one sweet cartridge package— he wants a bomb which will drop a grizzly if it

hits him in the toe. So he what? Better believe!
Comedy is the study of the unsound actions of
the cowardly under stress, just as tragedy is
equal study time of the brave under heroic but
enigmatic, reverberating, resonant conditions of
loss—yes, professor, you may keep the change,
for D.J. is, mean to say, *has* got more than a
finger into the cunt of genius, Madame Muse.
He has now to tell you that poor Very Low-
Grade Medium Asshole Pete is so squash-
breathed at the ups and downs of careerman-
ship and sudden death which now confront him
that he buys—get in line to look at it—from a
white-haired riverboat string-tie type of an ex
oil well promoter, some friend of his wife's shift-
less uncle's boss, a third-string Dallas Mafia type
(don't even look how that gun got around to
there or the Ford Foundation will be up and
along for gropes) this gun being a used, indeed
banged-up, African rhinoceros-hippo-elephant-
soften-the-bullet-for-the-lion double-barreled .600
–.577 custom, only-one-of-its-kind-ever-built Jeffrey Nitro Express carrying a 900-grain bullet
for Shot #1, a 750-grain for Shot #2, and a
recoil guaranteed to knock a grand piano on its
ass. Forget about the French walnut and the
Jeffrey action, the Hensoldt Zielklein 2¾× scope
interchangeable with the Redfield 2×-7× blunt

picket post with cross wire variable scope on the
Pachmayr Lo-Swing mount or the addition of
the Lyman aperture in the 17A front sight on
the .577 barrel to be used when the rhinoceros
is so close, friends, that the use of a telescopic
sight is not indicated (which means, Herbert,
that you better put the muzzle in your mouth
and blast that rhino horn right back out of your
ass). Yeah! This was the gun F. Lap-Ass Medium
Asshole Pete brought to Alaska for grizzly. When
he saw it, Rusty had a pure shit fit. If it hadn't
been a Jeffrey he'd have laughed his nuts off.
But, fix on this, Rusty thought he had the only
big bore Jeffrey in the State of Texas, and here
was his flunky with a bigger, and *double!* . .

"How'd you get this mother-fuck?" he asked
Pete. "I haven't heard of a double Jeff Nite Express since they used it to kill a Swiss dragon
who was terrorizing some Tyrolean village in
1921."

"Somebody sold it to me," Pete confesses.

"Well, I hope you didn't pay too much, because the fellow must have stolen it."

In fact, Pete has bought it for $1,000 heart-
hurting bucks. A swindle and a crime. The two
barrels are thus crooked they could shoot each
other. Pore Pete, Be Your Boss Pete, has had
already to lay out near to $4,200 bucks for this

Brooks Range safari-and-*gun* and has thus had to sell his #2 car, a somewhat used Jag XKE for three big ones plus another thou by converting some Dreyfus Fund into straight cash. He wouldn't dare sell his Pure Pores debentures, no, nor go further into installment debt.

Well, Rusty is in a marching state of perturbation. The very presence of that gun seems enough to shatter the tissue or texture of the spell which hangs over every happy hunter. Up in the basin, by the fire, night before the morning Tex killed the wolf, Big Luke has taken one look at Pete's possession and Rusty knows what he is thinking: this is one extrafine gaggle of goose fat and asshole to contend with for a week. So Rusty attacks. He knows enough to get attention off that Nitro Express! He inquires after Big Ollie's second gun, knowing pure well there is only the Remington 721, Big Ollie is a man for an all-purpose rifle, and when Big Luke says, "Ollie take care of everything with one gun," Rusty says, "Yeah, well why're you carrying a .375?"

"Ollie can back you up just as well with that .30-06."

"You know a .30-06 isn't going to do the job of a .375 Magnum. It wasn't *designed to*," says Rusty, getting a good old Texas range whine like the ricochet of a bullet off a stupid-ass Texas desert rock. He is obviously thinking of Mr. Grizzer. What Big Luke is thinking is not so far from conjecture. He is either (a) carrying a .375 to make his clients happy, since he shoots good enough to stop anything with a .30-06, a #.270, even a .245 if he got to, or (b) he has lost more nerve than Ollie, so he has more power in his fire stick. Either way, he got to protect Ollie and his one gun, he ain't getting in a situation where he might have to tell #2 man what sort of gun said #2 is supposed to sling in order to keep Sir Jet-Throne happy.

Rusty knows all this too, but he hasn't put in the years being a first-line Ranger Commando in 4C and P for zero return, he knows how to keep an expert on the defensive (and remind him of a nightmare or two) by poking in just hard enough to the mysteries between the facts. "Listen," says Rusty, "nobody knows finally what's going to kill big game. Some seem to go over if you put a pin in their butt, others you take right through the heart—they keep running. Running right at you if need be."

"Shoot for the shoulder, not the heart," says Big Luke in a voice like a piece of old oiled gunstock, a voice with a patina—he has said this two thousand times over the years.

"Right," says Rusty, "the shoulder. Break the shoulder bone, and they can't run. Sure. That's where I want my power. Right there. Right then. Maybe a professional hunter takes pride in dropping an animal by picking him off in a vital spot —but I like the feeling that if I miss a vital area I still can count on the big impact knocking them down, killing them by the total impact, shock! it's like aerial bombardment in the last Big War," he said, turning to Tex, D.J., and the Medium Assholes, and dropping his voice as if he were now imparting the flavor of the secret jellies and jams used in black mass of real military lore, "why, face up, gentlemen, the British were right, hear, hear, they were right for once, you don't pinpoint vital areas in a city, you blot it all out, you bury it deep in fire, shit, and fury. Then when the war's over they're glad to see you come in. It's just like if you get in a fight with a fellow, you're well advised to destroy him half to death. If y'get him down, use your shoe on his face, employ your imagination, give him a working-over, hard to believe, but often enough that man is your friend afterward, you've made him sane—maybe he thought before he had the fight with you he could lick whatever was in sight so he was half-crazy, now he knows that is not exactly so. Whereas if you give him a nice clean whipping, you've stimulated him to give you a nice clean whipping back. Of course, the analogy is not perfect, Luke, but I am forced to wonder about the fine difference in ethics between using Ollie's .30-06, and my Special .404, or your .375. Yes, it may be our animals will die a degree more from shock and a hint less from vital execution. But of what final ethical consequence is that, where is the fine difference?"

"Your meat tastes better when you're executed," said Tex.

Big Luke gave a laugh, Rusty gave a look at the undertaker's son. "Let me just tell you," he said into the fire, "I hope I don't have to stand on tiptoe too long waiting for you, Tex, to squeeze a needle out of your .270."

"You won't," said Tex.

Well, M.A. Pete heard all of this and more, he heard from his tentmate M.A. Bill a little later that night, for Bill was a ballistics nut and had spent one full vacation in the ballistics department of the FBI in the Department of Justice building in D.C. (having used the influence of his boss Death-row Jelly-Go Jet-Throne and the friendship of some of the local FBI to be accepted as a guest-visitor and temporary student on the comparative rank basis of police captain so that M.A. Bill got his studying in with visit-

ing foreigners like the head of the Ghana Police
Department, and the Mozambique Police Department, and native fuzz from Spokane, Walla
Walla, Greensboro—they were all taking the full
invitation and orientation course in updated
police detection methods, but M.A. Bill was no
investigator manqué, rather he was a ballistics
nut, and that's where he stayed for two hot
blazing summer weeks in the air-conditioned
laboratories of the ballistics boys). He'd always
gone in for handloading his cartridges, but when
he got back, he was abruptly become the cartridge expert in his rifle club cause he could advise you on the FBI selection and use of bullets,
primer, case, shot, and powder, he was up on
the latest Department of Justice methods of
determining chamber pressure, mean effective
pressure, hunting loads, reasonable uses for black
powder, new powders, flash holes, bullet cast-
ings, bullet swaging, etc., he had a spread of loading tools, dies, accessories, components, lathes,
and was therefore all equipped to wildcat his
own. Some of them were pretty hot. M.A. Bill
had been known to come into the office with
gunpowder injected in his pores, but a breech
had never blown up in his face. Of course, no
dentist has love for a doctor, and no wildcatter
has a good word for a factory cartridge. M.A.

Pete had been ready after Rusty's contumely to bury his Jeffrey Nitro Express and make the trip with the Savage 110 .30-06, but M.A. Bill squared him off on that. He let him in on the secret— factory ammunition was the unspoken scandal of American life, and .30-06, well in M.A. Bill's opinion, they were the worst offenders. The f.p.s. (foot per second, knothead!) variations had been known to go up to 5 percent, and one box in not that very many you'd be surprised had such variations and fluctuations in their max. vel., as tested on the chronograph that trajectories could even be affected. Which meant? Pete wanted to know. Errors in shooting, said M.A. Bill. D.J. is here to tell you that M.A. Pete wished to hear no more, which was error indeed, cause a little cross-examination would have revealed that M.A. Bill was talking about a difference which was not an inch at one hundred yards, not by half. You see, fellow Americans, statistics perverts, and number addicts, the greatest effect of varia- tion in powder loadings speaks up after you go by the sign which says, "You are a rifle bullet passing the three-hundred-yard mark and are bound soon to dip. Keep your nose up!" In fact, M.A. Bill like most ballistics nuts was as near- sighted as an old hound with silver rim lenses so his critique is academic for himself. He's not

interested in where the bullet goes, he just wants
to stuff it full of the right sort of smokeless. Love,
love, the Good Lord may have had no idea how
far he cast his seed.

"But your gun is a .30-06," says M.A. Pete.

"Yes, but I've had it rechambered and with a
custom barrel. I make my own shell for it. A
.311. I wouldn't ever use a .30-06."

"Oh," said Pete, "that .311 must really do the
job."

"You can go to sleep on that," said M.A. Bill.

M.A. Pete did not sleep too well. He had
visions of a grizzly bearing down on him with
a wild cry like a Nigger washerwoman gone ape
with a butcher knife, and he had seen himself
forced to face such music with the slim pencil
of a .30-06. He had had dreams of bringing it
off with a .30-06 but that buried scandal of
American sporting rifle cartridge ammo f.p.s.
discrepancies recounted to him by M.A. Bill had
the front sight of his Savage·110 wavering like
a fly wing in his mind's eye. If the aim of the
bullet could not be trusted, then of what purport
the gun? So, fuck if he didn't have his hand on
the double Jeffrey all night long and kiss your
own ass deep in the heart of Texas if the elephant gun wasn't the tool that M.A. Pete brought

with him when he went running down into the
valley and the green park of lawn below the
black-ass gray basin, down in the sweet green
grass right after Tex shot his wolf, that grass
green as an English lawn, just where the trees
ended and the mountain went up in a gray dome.
And standing around, looking at the dead wolf,
he looked up, and he, the medium asshole, was
the first to see a caribou two hundred yards
away through the thin trees, and in the accurate
fevered inaccuracy of being awake a night without sleep, he took a sight and the cross hairs on
the scope ran a figure eight around the horns,
which then plummeted down around the hooves,
flew up past the tail into the air, about, and back
over the caribou's flanks to a view, all abrupt,
honest, naked, and hairy of the buck's testicles
magnified $4\times$, which to M.A. Pete's unprotected
eye was equal in force and simple animal revela-
tion to the first sight provided an innocent
maiden of a workingman's balls, and then past
caribou's deer nuts in a blur as if M.A. Pete was
in a movie traveling the curves so it was all a
blur, and around came the sights again to the
back of the hocks and up and RUMBA! went the
Jeffrey and the .600 Nitro Express shot on its
way and M.A. Pete took a blow to the shoulder

on recoil which canted his vertebrae 3 degrees 21 minutes right then and there, and Wow! came a sound next to him, for the caribou leaped in the air, did a crazy dance, and was off in the woods.

★

===

INTRO BEEP 6

===

★

Well, D.J.'s consciousness must be expiring in the brackish backwaters of a sluggish narrative, for we have been hung up in numbers, details, and all sorts of overspecific technical data as if it were scum, slime, pollen slick, floating twigs, and wet rotting leaves all meandering down a dead-ass stream, but, man, you leave those paved streets and get your ass flown abruptly from the high technological nexus and overdeveloped civilization of a megacity like the Dallas–Fort Worth complex into a riptide impact and collision area marginated halfway between civilization and a nature culture-primitive constellation

(like Alaska, man) and then intensify such cul-
ture shock by inserting the subjects (1 H.A.,
2 M.A. and 2 TA½T)—which latter stands for
Tex and D.J. (2 Tough Adolescents ½ Tested)—
well, you might just as well sing along with the
Rotten Moss and the Red Hots, Yeah, I Got an
Itching in My Palm Which Some Call Love, because that's shock, Mr. Buzz-buzz, up from Dallas
into the Brooks Range, and boys like Rusty and
the M.A.s all being men, there's just nothing to
do with Mr. Anxiety but carry him around in
place of Herr Dread, and hang out those numbers, Harvey, don't forsake those names, Nelson,
remember that being up from Dallas so abrupt
makes a man feel small and modest like he's
full of shit, so give a little Christian bomb,
spelled b-a-l-m, and forgive and forget that slow
smelly backed-up hardly moving narrative stream
of facts, figures and general meaningless horseshit which D.J. has been feeding, and fix your
eye on the white stumpy tail and sweet white ass
of the buck caribou up and bounding away and
now the problem is to track him.

CHAP SIX

D.J., your presumptive philosopher, has not made the grand connection yet between the balls and the ears although he would claim they are related—more of this later, maybe—but the eyes are of course attached to the asshole as beginning is to end: the end is putting something out—the beginning is to see what you are going to have to shit out, and that right here in Brooks Range is easy to know because it will be the recollection of the blood on the cotton white ass of that caribou just hit by M.A. Pete. A liver-vitiating sight, Carter, for the liver goes flat, D.J. would assure you, whenever some scent meets its deodorant, or an herb is fed with aspirin. Pretty literary for adolescent out hunting with Paw? Go fuck, D.J.'s got his purchase on the big thing —genius—and he know this: you deaden a mystery and your liver goes to shit. This chase for a torn-ass caribou revolves around a simple mystery, to wit the ass of the caribou is white, its stumpy tail is white, soft as a white ruffle at Milady Hightits throat, so D.J. ask you why? Why is the rear view of a thousand head of caribou passing on the tundra like a thousand pops of cotton on the boll? That's a dead-ass question—the ass of your mind go dead trying to answer, yeah, and here was just one caribou, off on a split through the woods. But we all had one look, one crack of a look at something red and hanging bad and loose like a wattle from the white fur. Then we were all walking and jogging down an open aisle of moss-green grass to the spot in the timber two hundred fifty yards below where the deer had plunged in.

Blood for his trail, drops the size of every kind of coin, silver dollars up to florins, even—one the size of a small plate—brown blood already corrupted by a hive of near invisible devourers, insect shitters, chiggers and flies, one big Alaska bumblebee still alive on this cold early September morning, and the sun shining right in the blood with a thousand lights, or so it would look if you had your nose right there on the bloodied leaves close enough to that wet to think you were looking at neon signs, the woods were full of awe, nothing other, the trees standing numb, cowardly spectators, man, watching one of their own take a wasting.

Then the trail of the blood took a bend, beat through dwarf alder, and some nasty kind of brush with too much in the way of catbriers. That took quite a few minutes, then a pine grove, then another aisle between trees, parallel to the one we had come down, but now the caribou trail was rising up to timberline again, and in the distance, up along a thousand yards, was what looked to be the caribou, yes, it was, and through the field glasses Big Luke, watching, shook his head. "You hit him an outside rump shot, Pete."

"Then he'll be all right?"

"No, impact seems to have broke his leg or maybe shocked his spine. He's using only one hind leg. Walking not much faster than us. That's bad. We can't leave him."

"Say," said Pete, trying to shift the rump of the subject, "why'd that buck leave timber?"

"Didn't want to die in those woods. Sometimes you get a buck will cross three open ridgelines

to get into the particular woods where he wants
to hide or give it up."

"Then he ain't too bad if he can move that
much."

"He," said Big Luke, "is bad enough that we
got to get him."

It was going to take all day. We were going
to spend our first day walking and jogging to
chase a wounded caribou, when there were ten
thousand head of them in the Brooks Range. All
honors due to M.A. Pete's Jeffrey Nitro Express.
Well, Luke got the helicopter up. It had been
down in Fairbanks for repair the day before, he
had not mentioned how near it was to reach,
oh no, he did not want to have Rusty on his ear
all those hours of the packtrain up the mountain
from Dolly Ding Bat Lake, but now he took us
up the aisle through the trees till we were above
timber again and led us along a shallow canyon
and over a saddle into our basin, and there while
breakfast was made by one of the flunky packer
guide cooks, Ed Smith, an Indian, Big Luke got
a big-ass walkie-talkie 3200 RS-1A 16 mile range,
and rang down to camp at the lake telling them
to come on in, and when they did with a smack
of static, he told them to bring the helicopter
on up.

That's how they got Kid Caribou. Helicopter

pilot was there in five minutes with Buster
Bubbletop, a real wasp of a Bell helicopter, and
Big Luke got in with M.A. Pete and M.A. Pete's
cannon, and they zipped up and over the ridge,
and Rusty, and Tex, and D.J. went to the top of
a knoll and followed them with Rusty's Hurdle &
Reuss 7 × 35 and Tex and D.J.'s own Jap Titan
8 × 35 and Binolux 7 × 35. And, man, this is
what they see—half dead ass caribou climbing
up those rocks, nice head of antlers (look to be
fourteen points through the glass) and a bleeding
jagged gored red ass, flap of flesh now wide open,
and the caribou makes those rocks with lunge
and grunt and like then a whimper you could
hear almost through the binocs when the sound
of the helicopter began to beat on caribou ear
with rings of ether just as when you going out
on the operating table. Man, that caribou looks
as dogged and frantic as a prospector climbing
a mountain to get a hill of gold, and then the
helicopter is on top of him and hovering and
holding him frozen, and it lands not fifty feet
away, and the caribou turns his ass and starts to
climb up a cliff with a set of deliberate steps like
(1) fuck you, (2) go kill, (3) shit on you, each
step a pure phrase of the blues—take me away,
Mr. Dixieland—and there is M.A. Pete stepping
out gingerly from the copter, like, man, he's

close to the caribou, and got his cannon with
him, and just as Old Buck Broken Ass gets to
the top of his little cliff, hopping slow on three
legs, M.A. Pete sends a Nitro Express up into
his gut from the rear, right into the red mask
of the old wound and that animal does a
Geländesprung right into the air as if his spine
is illumined in incandescence, and somersaults
in the air, and falls twenty feet from the cliff,
smashing one set of antlers off his head (to be
wired on later, nothing other) and the .600 900-
grain blasted through his intestines, stomach,
pancreas, gallbladder, liver and lungs, and left
a hole to put your arm in, all your arm, up to
the shoulder if you are not squeamish, entrail
swimmer, and then bullet breaking, some of the
fragments ripped into the brain and out the
head, leaving it scarred to the point where M.A.
Pete could claim (and believe) two years later
that the scars on the mouth and face of his deer
trophy were the fighting marks of a big buck
caribou fighter; other fragments sawed through
the ribs of the lungs, and deteriorated like buck-
shot in the forequarter. Big Luke brought that
animal back to feed us. Its guts, belly and lungs
were one old jelly flung together by the bullets,
one blood pudding of a cocktail vibrated into
total promiscuity by the twenty-foot fall down

the rocks. Yes, prince, yes, Big Luke got the
head off, and rescued the loose antler, and
gutted the entrails, dressed the meat to clean
fragments, left the hide which was a mess—
clear surprise, yes!—but we had the meat for
lunch, and it wasn't exactly gamy, it tasted loud
and clear of nothing but fresh venison steeped
in bile, shit, and the half-digested contents of a
caribou's stomach—it was so bad you were living
on the other side of existence, down in poverty
and stink wallow with your nose beneath the
fever—that was Luke's message to us.

The helicopter was new to him, you read, and
for some parties in the last year or so he'd begun
to use it, for some not, but he was an American,
what the fuck, he had spent his life living up
tight with wilderness and that had eaten at him,
wilderness was tasty but boredom was his cor-
ruption, he had wanted a jolt, so sees it D.J.,
Big Luke now got his kicks with the helicopter.
He was forever enough of a pro not to use it
with real hunters, no, man, but he had us, gaggle
of goose fat and asshole, killers of bile-soaked
venison, so the rest of the hunt, all next seven
days he gave what was secretly wanted, which
was helicopter heaven, and it was curious shit,
all rules and regulations, for of course we did not
hunt from the air, no freakmen from TV land

us, but rather noble Dallasassians, so we broke open a war between us and the animals, and the hunt hills of the Moe Henry and Obungekat Safari patch rang with ball's ass shooting, the real breeze, hopping to the top of a mountain on copter wings to shoot down on goats, nothing so great as the Alaska mountain goat, yeah, you get up at three A.M. in tent camp up high above timber, and you climb, man, on foot above timber, for three hours till dawn, and then climb higher still crabbing up sixty-degree rock slopes, and walking with all heart shit up in your throat along a ledge twelve inches or less, yeah, ooh, making it up, and higher still, *quietly*, and then if you good, you're up there, up above Master Mountain Goat, and when you start to shoot on him, he does a step dance like an old Negro heel-and-toe tap man falling down stairs or flying up them, and the first animal D.J. got in Alaska was a mountain goat at two hundred and fifty yards, and with one shot, animal stood on its nose for one long beast of a second, and then did a running dying dance for fifty yards down the rocks like a fakir sprinting through flaming coals, and when he died, *Wham!* the pain of his exploding heart shot like an arrow into D.J.'s heart, and the animals had gotten him, they were talking all around him now, communicating the

unspoken unseen unmeasurable electromagnetism
and wave of all the psychic circuits of all the
wild of Alaska, and he was only part of them,
and part he was of gasoline of Texas, the asshole
sulfur smell of money-oil clinging to the helicopter, cause he had not gotten that goat by
getting up in the three A.M. of morning and
climbing the mountain, no cream not your dear
private lace, dear Celia, D.J. had gotten up at
seven back in the bunkhouse at Dolly Ding Bat
Lake, for once Big Luke had decided this was
Helicopter Week for Goose Fat Gaggle, he
bundled all souls and A-holes back to the bunkhouse since good old Hail the Cop Turd could
take you a day's walk in ten minutes, and he
would drop us on spots, top of a mountain, edge
of a bull moose pond, across a canyon from Dall
ram, near a feeding ground for the grizzer, that
copter was dividing us up, carrying us here, there,
every which spot, shooting in parties of two and
four, guide and guest, or two guides, two guests,
and it was a haul of big-ass game getting, for
among the five of us safari payers we had a limit
of twenty-five assorted grizzly, moose, ram, goat
and caribou, and there was animal steaks being
cut and packed all over the place, and trundled
out by copter back to Dolly Ding Bat and up
again in Super Cub to Fairbanks and freezers,

all that hot supersensitive game meat now locked
in brown paper and stone ice, paralyzed stiff in
a freezer, about to suffer for sins it could not
locate, yes, that was how D.J. got his mountain
goat, he was flown at seven in the morning up to
the top of a spiky ridge not too unlike the moon,
set down in a bowl with Tex, Ollie, and Kenny
Easterly, and waited, and in two hours had his
shot, had his action, climbing down a ravine,
and up the other side, a walk of four hundred
yards, had his work helping Big Ollie skin,
butcher, gut and package Mr. Goat (being shown
by Ollie how to keep the fur away from the
meat so the taste would not be tainted—touch of
goat skin on raw goat meat smelling as stale
and raunchy as overworked whore) and then
Big Ollie having radioed the copter, in came the
Hail the Cop and let down a line all hovering
and they slung the meat packages, and the horns
and head onto the lift line, which pulled it up
and then pulled them up—that was the kick of
the morning, foot in the stirrup, lifting one
hundred feet to the Cop Turd which vibrated
above like one giant overgrown Hog! its car-
buretor farting, its motor giving out that family
sputter of gasoline being piston-cooked at medium speed, but D.J. never looked at the head of
the goat except once, for the goat had a clown's

expression in his little-ass red dying eyes, the fires of the heart working to keep custard on the clown's face, it wasn't until that night when he was in the bunkhouse back at Dolly Ding Bat that D.J. relaxed enough to remember that goat picking his way up and down rocks like a slow motion of a skier through slalom, his legs and ass swinging opposite ways, carefree, like take one leg away, I'll do it on the other, and it hit D.J. with a second blow on his heart from the exploding heart of the goat and he sat up in bed, in the bunk, listening to the snores, stole out to the night, got one breath of the sense of that *force* up in the North, of land North North above him and dived back to the bed, his sixteen-year-old heart racing through the first spooks of an encounter with Herr Dread.

What more you want to hear? They got them all, crazy caribou trophy heads, eighteen-point buck for M.A. Bill, M.A. Bill! his handload .311 cartridge did the job, and tore off the ass—D.J. will not dwell on why an asshole is bound to hit the ass, for that is homeopathic magic, man—we got it all, that helicopter made us like a bee pulling honey from flower after flower, moose and goose if there'd been goose, and Dall ram, horns and horns of Dall ram, all five of us in three teams got to blast our own set of horn be-

fore one day was done on a herd up in a sink
near a pinnacle, and Big Luke's Cop Turd pilot
was pushing the rules and regs of Hail Cop hunting, for after he lower us out on the line which
had even Rusty close to involuntary defecation
(and was the most heroic thing corporation execs
have done in many a year), why, we got left set
up two hundred yards from old herd of Dall ram,
Mr. and Mrs. Beautiful Ibex horn (that's Jew
horn, I Beck'n Son, hih, hih) ain't got the curl
and spiral of the universe curving out of their
brain for nothing, they took up and off, and Mr.
Cop Turd went swinging after them like a darn-
ing needle after ladybugs and headed the Dall
ram off till they started to run back toward us,
at which point he cut them off again (by crossing
in front of them only thirty feet above—kick
hump in this hunting is: be Cop pilot) since unwritten Copt. rules and regs forbid chasing of
game into gun, at which point Dall ram leader
was like to be very confused and hit out this
way and that way, and the Cop just went circling
around until the sheep were fixed, shit they were
hypnotized, it was pretty to watch, cause Hail
Cop was like a bullfighter twisting a bull through
the limits of his neck until he just got to stand
and wait and let his neck recover, and the copter
having the herd of Dall ram finally fixed on a

cleft in a ridge across a bare modest draw from us, us hiding in the rocks on the lip of the sink, he pulled up and out, each circle a little bigger than the one before, and now a little higher until the animals shivering from the release of anxiety, in fact all strung out from the sound of air boiling, breaking, roaring and tearing and the whine —what cry of what beast?—were able to do no more than walk around, hocks trembling, muzzles nuzzling assholes—like get back to that flesh, man! they must have felt they were being born out again.

I got the first shot. Kneeling behind a rock with a moss hummock not larger than the hand for a rest, it all felt good, I had gotten so hypnotized myself, there was no fever looking through the scope, the eye picked on one ram standing on one rock all four legs together and head silhouetted out against a sawtooth ridge maybe five miles behind him, and in the scope I had one look at the prettiest face D.J. has ever seen, almond oval and butter love for eyes, a little black sweet pursed mouth, all quivering now, two nostrils cunning as an old Negro witch smelling gypsy money on a mark, whoo-ee—I got the dot above my reticule in the center of the curl of the horn—those horns went three hundred and sixty degrees around the ear, like holding

the mountain in the palm of your hand, they
were receptors to hear the curve of the wind in
the private cave of the mountains about, they
were a coil of horn around the nerve which tunes
the herb, and D. Ramses was all horned in on
me, hair to the left, hair to the right went his
head, we could just as well have been pulling
opposite ends. I could not help it, wanting to
keep that head intact for a trophy, the scope still
would not leave the horn, the dot stayed on the
ram brain, one inch above the eye, and feeling
like the instant before the jump first time off a
garage roof, D.J. pulls his trigger finger, perfect
pull, perfect shot, as if all spiral of horn was
funnel to pull all of the aim in and the shot
went in one inch above the eye and the animal
went down like a wall had fallen, best shot D.J.
ever made, and Rusty rushed in his shot, cause
his sheep took off at D.J.'s shot, Rusty only
wounded his beast, got a second blast away too
high in the shoulder, off with a third in the hoof
—believe it if you want—the hoof later as splat-
tered from the .404 as a wad of tar beaten with
a hammer, and finally got him in the shoulder
near the heart, the animal not moving hardly
now, was Rusty mad. Four .404s for a Dall ram
(he not carrying #2 gun or #3, cause who
knows where grizzly might be?). If he needed

four for the ram, maybe four times four for the bear.

More skinning, more packing, two great trophy heads, and a wait for the helicopter out servicing Tex and M.A.s Pete-Bill. They all had Dall ram that day. Five sets of horns held in the arms of five shit-eating grins standing in semicircle on the banks of Dolly Ding Bat Lake as the pictures were taken, and long careful discussions with Big Luke on taxidermy and where the Moe Henry and Obungekat Safari Group recommended the preservation of the head—any fifty-year guarantee outfits around, or century mounters? "There's no real craftsmen left," says M.A. Pete. "Just embalmers," said Tex.

Going for the grizzer wasn't nearly so good. Mr. Cop Turd, carrying Rusty, M.A. Bill, and Ollie, went flying by one pure grizzly standing out in an alpine meadow out on a flank of mountain where the spruce grew up in columns like the teeth of a comb and they had been swinging so good knocking down trophies that Rusty got Napoleonic, rode his luck all the way to Veneria and back, and made the pilot set them down two hundred meager yards away, which is to say he put Rusty out first at Rusty's demand, Rusty going down the winch, that two hundred yards' separation from the bear not very much

when you're waiting for the guide and your
rifle buddy to follow, but no choice, the alpine
meadow was small, so there was Rusty on the
ground alone unslinging his Jeffrey, all alone
when the bear instead of deciding to meander
away from the helicopter and the man, or take
a long-distance look, came bearing instead into
them with a roar—hours later D.J. could still hear
it echoing out of the ashy pores of Rusty's mon-
umentally shaken skin. Well, Mr. Cop Turd
wasn't waiting for Rusty to down that grizzer
standing in an alpine meadow all alone, no, they
were not going to let any bear hang a human
trophy in his den, not at the expense of the Moe
Henry Group. Hail the Cop jammed his whirlybird right down on a line toward the bear
charging so near overhead that the bear reached
up with his paws and took a mighty swipe, at
which point Rusty got a shot off, a decent shot,
decent enough to miss the copter by as much as
it missed the bear, and sound of the shot, Old
Grizzer split ass for the woods, while Cop-bird
whirlybird came back and picked up Old Rust—
Old Zinc White ex Rusty Jethroe—even the shit
hue in his eyes pale as junket, and back they
went to the bunkhouse. Discussion that night.
Rusty was sick. He had to get it up. They had
to go for grizzer now. Well, he was man enough

to steel his guts before necessity, he not D.J.'s
father for naught tickle, D.J. was conceived in
deep waters. So Rusty agreed in his own heart
to get it up. Now he's awake, man, lying in his
bunk looking out a small six-pane window at
moonlight on the lake, and the smell of the pine
grove around the bunkhouse is strong, it speaks
of Indian caverns, of forest no white man ever
saw, which is to say it smells like no pine forest
Rusty ever saw, for the odor goes in and in again
until he is afraid to breathe all the way, aisles
are opening in his brain before the incense of it
which is like the odor of the long fall in a dream.
Blasts of rage and gouts of fear burn like jets
and flush like bile waters and he is humped in
his mind on Hallie, D.J.'s own father, Rusty,
married twenty years to a blond beauty he can
never own for certain in the flesh of his brain.

INTRO BEEP 7

Yeah, the time is soon coming, thinks Rusty, when fornication will be professional athletics, and everybody will watch the national eliminations on TV. Will boys like D.J. and Tex be in the finals with a couple of Playboy bunnies or black ass honeys? well, shit-and-sure, fifty thousand major league fuckers will be clawing and cutting to get in the big time to present their open flower petal pussy, or hand-hewn diamond tool and testicles in happy magnification by Color Vision RCA. Only thing holding this scheme back is the problems of integration. What if the Spades run away with the jewels?

Not to mention all the wet pussy in America.
Think of that in Color TV—all the purple majesty, hey says Rusty, if they do, America'll really
be looking for a white hope, huh.

Of course, thinks Rusty, I'll be having to watch.
Oh, the ignominy. Just stick my middle-age dick
against the screen. Yeah, sighs Rusty, the twen-
tieth century is breaking up the ball game, and
Rusty thinks large common thoughts such as
these: (1) The women are free. They fuck too
many to believe one man can do the job. (2) The
Niggers are free, and the dues they got to be
paid is no Texas virgin's delight. (3) The Niggers and the women are fucking each other. (4)
The Yellow races are breaking loose. (5) Africa
is breaking loose. (6) The adolescents are breaking loose including his own son. (7) The European nations hate America's guts. (8) The
products are no fucking good anymore. (9) Communism is a system guaranteed to collect dues
from all losers. (9a) More losers than winners.
(9b) and out: Communism is going to defeat
capitalism, unless promptly destroyed. (10) a.
Fucking is king. b. Jerk-off dances are the royal
road to the fuck. c. Rusty no great jerk-off dancer.
d. Rusty disqualified from playing King Fuck.
(11) The white men are no longer champions in
boxing. (12) The great white athlete is being

superseded by the great black athlete. (13) The
Jews run the Eastern wing of the Democratic
party. (14) Karate, a Jap sport, is now pre-
requisite to good street fighting. (15) The sons
of the working class are running around America
on motorcycles. (16) Church is out, LSD is in.
(17) He, Rusty, is fucked unless he gets that
bear, for if he don't, white men are fucked more
and they can take no more. Rusty's secret is that
he sees himself as one of the pillars of the firma-
ment, yeah, man—he reads the world's doom in
his own fuckup. If he is less great than God
intended him to be, then America is in Trouble.
They don't breed Texans for nothing. Rusty has
a great philosophy, states D.J., it is just you have
to be an honest son of a bitch to make it work,
for—peer into this—you're the fulcrum of the
universe, right? the good Lord takes his reading
off you, right? (Rusty figures—D.J. will tell you
—that the Lord despising mass methods does not
bother to weigh man in the aggregate or the
mass; instead he stays close to a chosen few,
and they ain't Hebes, Rusty hopes to tell you)
so Rusty being the cat off whom the reading is
read, being that fundament of mind, flesh, and
being whose moves are intimate to the Lord, he
got to be honest with himself if he want to be
on fulcrum point, because if he think he's doing

good, and the good Lord knows he's not, well, kiss your own sweet ass, Eustachia, Rusty is then no longer up tight with G.O.D.—Grand Old Divinity (biggest corporation of them all? Rusty often thinks not) no, you are one place, God is another, how can you serve? But then an asshole, even a H.G. asshole, cannot be honest by definition, for it would claim to be an organ like any other, it would pretend to have no guilt, and yet it fumes, man. Ho, ho, wait and see.

CHAP SEVEN

Big Luke and Kenny Easterly were not running velvet guided tours of America's last unspoiled wilderness for naught tickle either, so they decided to have the whole group together on the grizzer hunt, five guests, four guides, and Mr. Guide Pilot in Cop-Bird Seat, Al Bell was his name flying a Bell 47J, three passengers, one pilot—take a bow—Al Bell, no relation to Bell 47J.

Big Luke had a military decision. Whether due to the atom bomb or to Al Bell and his 47J and numerous other yclepts helicopts from Sam Sting Safari, and other Safari Counters with their respective airplanes, Cop Turds, and general fission of the psychomagnetic field (new concept, Suck-Mouth) of the wild life in the Brooks Range, the fact is that the grizzers had gone ape. Big Luke had known grizzers all his life—there was a time when he knew them so well he could walk up to a peaceful one and pat him on the shoulder, the bear ain't an undivided heavy, a stone sadist, no, grizzer can be patted on the back, at least was a time but now the psycho-magnetic field was a mosaic, a fragmented vase as Horace said to Ovid, and Big Luke couldn't be sure if he was still in contact with his monu-mental cool, too many grizzers were charging the hunter before the first shot. So Big Luke took a military fix. He had two adolescents who could shoot *maybe*, and one high-grade asshole who could shoot some of the time, and two M.A.s who had a fifty-fifty even locating a moving tar-get in their scope. He had the guides of course, he could count on his guides, they would hold, they would keep shooting until the bear's breath was up their nose, but the clients had to get the first shot (with any pretense of class, the second as well) so look, here's a grizzer, wounded twice, a mind now halfway between dragon and dino-saur, fire in his gut, lightning in his shoulder, and zero in his life but heart, teeth, fangs, get those long claws in, and Luke's guide waiting

for client to get two shots off now has the
Grizzly Express running straight on them, not
forty yards away, hop, lurch, leap, heave. For
those forty yards the grizzer could be fast as a
mustang. Even if guide hits him three times
more, maybe grizzer doesn't stop until he takes a
human trophy out with him into the twilight
beyond the painted waters. "Ah swan," says Big
Luke, "my client died in the old bear's arms."
Shit! That cannot be. Big Luke has never lost a
client, but there are averages, laws, and retribu-
tion. Cop Turds are exploding psychic ecology
all over the place, and this is above the *Circle*,
man, every mind, human, animal, even vegetable,
certainly mineral (crystal mineral) is tuned in
to the same place, wait and see, better believe,
Big Luke knows he's getting away with too
much, he's violating the divine economy which
presides over hunters, and so he could lose a
client, he would mar the record of a life, this is
Yukon, man, heroes fall, listen to Big Luke folklore, Big Ruby Lil, the great whore of Saskatche-
wan, never failed to please a client, giants and
pygmies they all came—Luke could tell the tale
—until the day she pressed her luck, took Yukon
hashish—what?—to speed the passing of the hours,
and behold an auditor from Manitoba rolled in
her comfortable soft brown slightly charred (from

thirty years of peter burn) sweet whore's old
Cadillac of a cunt, it was thus big and roomy
(the secret was that her clients used to let the
fatigue of a lifetime shoot, fire or seep out into
those homey cunt walls—she was medicine, man)
well, the audit got it up but he could not let it
go, there was a knot of congested fatigue in his
heart, he was afraid he would blast himself if he
ever blew it into her, so Ruby Lil tried everything, she even, after four hours, sucked his dick,
and Ruby Lil had not done that for twenty years,
she was a Mexico-Eskimo Queen, man, she put
down the taste of semen, but she even did the
rim on that auditor with the eyeglasses from
Manitoba, yet she failed, he never got the first
drop to say sayonara to his dick, no floods of
seed left the comptometer of his nuts, and Ruby
Lil declined and was diminished to a dyke.

This Big Luke's thoughts? No, it's D.J. on the
edge of masturbating in the Alaska night, with
the excitement of going for griz in the morning,
and holding off, holding off, cause a handful of
spit on a sixteen-year-old dick puts a worm on
the trigger and you slip off your shot.

This is defalcation from the point. Big Luke
is also lying awake, and the knot of fatigue in
the auditor from Manitoba's heart which D.J. is
cooking via his fantasy is the actual knot of tired

Herr Dread in Big Luke's heart (how's that for symbology, syph-head?). Yeah, now. So Big Luke General Fellinka makes his military disposition. They must be in position to bomb and superblast any grizzer who attacks. Therefore they will all make it together—five clients, five guides, Luke knows the spot, there's the bank of a mud-lick where berries grow—but the nightmare persists. Military solutions proliferate new problems, Pierrot. If General Luke has his double line of infantry, five clients in a straight row with five guides behind, just let one grizzer break through the line, and clients will be shooting at each other and at guides, what embroilment! no, the bank of the mud-lick is out, he'll have to form a circle around a knoll, and pictures of terrain circulate his head, revolve, come to a stop, start up again.

Big Luke finally picked the patch. It was a chimney of vertical rock round about one hundred feet in diameter, and bushes at its base where hunters could fire from cover. It stood in the middle of one emerald alpine meadow far enough beneath timber to hope and expect for more than one or two bear, and patches of buffalo berry and blueberry showed at the edge of the trees. Luke disposed his Hot-Shot Special as follows: ten men including himself set out in

an arc one-third of the way around the chimney
on the side facing those berry bushes (upwind
side) and he pinned the line with two guides at
each end. Five hunters and himself in the middle. By that method, the fire of two guides
would impact on any bear circling around the
flank from the blind side of the chimney, and
the cross fire of all four guides ready to concen-
trate on any one bear attacking anywhere up the
middle. If the bear ever reached the center, Luke
knew he there to be the man to stop it. Thus
disposition is done. General Luke Fellinka now
trundled the Pure Pores boys and Moe Henry
guides in by copter to a knoll one mile away
and then walked them over open country, high
on the ridgeline, so no bear could pop in on
them in the brushwood.

All set up, Big Luke made a speech. "Don't
hold fire too much! Any bear you see belongs to
all of you. You can all shoot. That's the way to
take him out." Shadow of Ruby Lil passes all
unseen over Big Luke's brainpan.

"Who does the bear belong to?" asks Rusty.

"I'll know," said Big Luke. "I can tell if the
first shot should get the credit, or if it belongs
to a later shot when that's the one does the
work."

Well, they didn't have too much to wait. Ninety

minutes later, about eleven in the morning, two
bears wandered into the meadow, husband and
wife but for the lack of a J.P., and the wind came
across the meadow from them sailing with such
connubial grizzly funky strength that Tex swore
afterward he could smell the bear on the breeze,
and that was why he saw them first. Tex got off
his shot first—it was his hunt this year—the male
was dead with a .270 through the brain, and
Rusty and Pete fired off two shots each at the
other bear who let loose a roar like the explosion
in the foghorn of a small-town firehouse when
the noon alarm goes off. And then she turned
and smashed off into the woods, blood all over
her back and flank, and was hit eight more times
by the guides, and dropped not ten yards back
into the trees.

Big Luke gave the award to M.A. Pete. The
second bear was Pete's bear, decided Luke. Pete
was ready to give it all to Rusty, and his cannon
too, but Luke after leading Rusty, Pete, Tex, and
a couple of guides up to Tex's bear (proved to
be stone dead on approach by failing any quiver
when stones were tossed at him) now walked
on, rifle at the hip, following the trail of the
female whose blood was red on the alders and
the dwarf birch trees, blood looking to expire
into brown gum on the pine needles still bright

as electric red on the cedar leaves, that red vibrating up D.J.'s nose in the cool gray blue ass sky green gray ground of Northland, up above the Circle, red above the Circle, red in the cool September Arctic air. Some giant wolf in D.J.'s heart, some prehistoric wolf all eight feet big began to stir new boils and springs and pools in the river of D.J., in his blood, beasty audience, in his blood, and he had to get him a wolf in the form of a bear like the grizzly bear plugged with twelve shots which lay there still shaking and broken and dead but still twitching, that female bear her belly half demolished by the Nitro Express of Medium Asshole Assistant to Procurement Manager Pure Pores Pete. Yeah. Rusty's shot had broken the shoulder and prob-ably carried near the heart, but Pete got the duke. "I think this bear went from massive shock," said Big Luke, hardly able to hold back a mas-sive shocker of a shit-eating grin. "Yours was nice shooting, Rusty—" dig—first time Luke calls Sir Jet-Throne, Rusty "—but Pete did the real job, so I'd call it."

Pete began to think of moving to Kansas City. That corporation land is mother, father, children, wife, hot weekend fuck, and romantic sorrow all in one. There are corporation execs who have sensibility fine as Anna K.'s (Anna Karenina, hunk-head!) for one thing: their boss. They know when their boss has ceased to love them. M.A.s in corporation land are vacuum tubes, man, ideal diodes, they are there to damp the waves in one direction, send them out the other, yes, yes, and cut out all the no no no. How else a boss to build up potential to transmit his communications without a M.A. vacuum tube or two in his network, Fergus? Well, the filament just burned out on Pete's tube. Ideal diode is no more.

"Where are you going to get that bear stuffed, Pete?" said Rusty.

"What do you recommend, Rusty?"

"Shoot another bear so you can patch the holes in this one."

What a cunt of a remark! But Rusty's got cunt in him. Vicious little streak he passed right on intact to D.J. Rusty don't look like Henry Cabot Lodge for nothing, he's already up and about and looking forward. Cause if he don't get a bear now, he can transfer to Japan.

Well, so there they go, right back to the chimney. And they wait for more bear. And more bear ain't coming. Bear may have gone ape shit in the Brooks Range, but they are not kamikaze, they can smell their own bear gum blood on the evergreen needles, and smell the insects strumming out all kinds of electronic ax music while insect pissing and shitting and orgy blood fucking with the flies in the wet red on the meadow and the woods, yeah, and those bears can smell the last shit blasted out of dead female grizzer with twelve slugs in her, and the shit that is ejected after death has passed through the vale and got an odor of the other, of the tomb, like the odor of cigarette breath on the mouth of a bitch who smokes forty cigs a day, you know the smell that goes back to Egypt. No bear comes. Not all the rest of that day, and back again in the morning, not all the rest of the next day. Next day Tex and M.A. Pete go off with guides to look for moose, Cop Turd is carrying them to a good shallow moose lake, and Rusty and D.J. are left with M.A. Bill and his Boom Boom Boomerang .311 Genius Special. It's amazing what waiting can do to a man's guts. M.A. Bill gets dreamy. He ceases to desire bear. Rusty scurries about in his gut and reamasses his cool. He is getting to feel taut and not without his ready—D.J. is more so than a young assassin with a knife. He too has got to get grizzer. The wolf is burning fever in him now, best future of his blood is going to boil off if he can't get on a bear (for he was the only one not to shoot at the female grizzer)—he had (tell it not even to

127

thine own armpit)—he had blown up in bull
buck bear fever. Or maybe it was all that jack-
off tension over Ruby Lil, yeah. The scope had
done a wiggle, finger did the trigger in a jig
and never pulled at all. So he is in the heart of
horror, he and Rusty can sit no longer in the
brush at the foot of the chimney looking at a
lazy meadow where no bear comes to feed on
berries, and the only sight in an hour is a loon
winging on south from high overhead. They
could be as well out in Texas desert as in this
gray ass Arctic Circle with its emerald green
lawns and the itch-dick memory of electric red
on the leaves. So they push on Luke to go out
tracking for bear, to push any direction into the
wind down trails through woods, fuck the cau-
tions, Rusty is indicating to Luke, let them be
hunters at last and take a trek for game. And
Luke resists, just as long as he can, he resists,
for the word is out to the grizzers on the Brooks
Range, this piece of patch anyway—and there's
sullen babies inside those bear hides now, they
could make an Ace Delinquent on a bad Spade
drunk seem like Angel Enlightenment next to
the look building in those itty-bitty mean grizzer
eyes. "Shit, man," said Rusty finally, "I'm taking
D.J. here and we are going to walk all fifteen miles
back to Ding Bat and see if we can't encounter

what we came to find." And Luke is wishing he had given the hide to Rusty.

Well, naught tickle to fare, Big Luke radios Cop Turd and tells him they're coming in on foot, and he'll give him another toodle-oo in two hours forty, and they string out now, Ed Smith the guide at point, Rusty, D.J., M.A. Bill and Big Luke. D.J. is finally walking with a gun across some miles of terrain in the Endicott Mountains of the untapped last wilderness Brooks Range.

And it's not that wild, man, it's not jungle, icicles, glaciers, mountain peaks, abysses, no, man, this patch right by to them here is nearly like Switzerland, but stretched out, baby, hint of big stuff, frozen ass snow peaks to the north, howlers of wind in the big cavities of the big mountains, but here it's just as clear and clean as a tasty blond fuck, I mean D.J. could say you might just as well be in Yosemite, Evan, you can't beat this land for long big clean cool, evergreens, man, the odor of evergreens pervadeth.

But Rusty is half-insane by now. That odor of evergreen might just as well be poppers for his inflamed brain. He ain't trundling his ass for two hours forty in order for Big Luke to radio the Cop Turd and taxi them in, he's not there to have his lust blooded and placated, he is up, his guts are there. So he turns to D.J. and says, "Son, let's split from Luke the Fink cause he ain't going to get your ass or mine near a grizzer." And D.J. who has been feeling the high hairy cool of a terrible turn where your short will hold or not hold old bitch road, it's endless, yes, that moment has been riding the next moment every step of their walk, he don't know if he's going to be a hero or dead, but he loves his daddy this instant, what a fuck of a stud, they will take off together, they will make their own way back to Camp, and Big Luke will sweat a huge drop. So in a turn around a ledge in the woods, they bear off sharp right, climb the ledge, let the others pass beneath, and work fast in the other direction, running when they are out of sight. Maybe they have run up a distance of a half mile in the woods before Big Luke will be aware they are gone, and Big Luke will work a quarter-mile circle for an hour at least before he decides they have dumped him. At which point they will be two miles away, and Rusty thereupon sprints off with D.J., making real rough woodsman time through these woods, easy going, lots of carpet, very still, little animals scattering, Northern cool slowly settling. They are off on a free, father and son.

★

INTRO BEEP 8

★

The pure moment of salt forming the crystal of this narrative going through D.J.'s super-accelerated consciousnes at eighteen right here and now when he sitting at the dinner table in the Dallas ass manse with Mr. Rusty Smoking Jacket, Halleloo all beautiful perfumed tits popping big tasty hostess heaves and Tex across from him, D.J.'s mother humping up secret heart of pussy welter wallow and slide tug suck fuck for Tex's nineteen-year-old dick, Tex, D.J.'s best friend, blood brother, incest is electric man, never forget, and eighteen between D.J. and Rusty it is all torn, all ties of properly sublimated parental-filial libido have been X-ed out man, die, love, die in a diode, cause love is dialectic, man, back and forth, hate and sweet, leer-love, spit-tickle, bite-lick, love is dialectic, and corporation is DC, direct current, diehard charge, no dialectic man, just one-way street, they don't call it Washington D.C. for nothing, eighteen, it's all torn, torn by the inexorable hunt logic of the Brooks Range when D.J. was sixteen, wait and see. Here they go. Here is the result of Rusty losing female grizzer with twelve male plugs from I don't know how many shooting tubes, think of fighting over a trophy which is as unknowing of its killer as the poor town fuck must be unknowing of the parental origins of her latest feet-ass (and head) now in embryo in her womb, forgive D.J. for acting like Dr. James Joyce, all junkies are the same, you know. Follow the hunt.

CHAP EIGHT

Rusty has been studying the map. He and D.J. are map readers (at your service, coordinates) and compass hounds. He even bought D.J. a Keuffel & Esser surveyor's transit, tripod, and tape for his fourteenth birthday. He knows they now have eleven miles to make before dark and five to six hours to do it in—long twilight still, endless ass of ass-end summer long Alaskan twilight, and he's not worried a bit at that, he's free, man, loose, loose as Henry with a goose, shedding those corporation layers, all that paper ass desk shit and glut, dictating larynx ass machines, six-button Tphones, buzzer shit (con-

ference table alcohol—where is your buzz), dead-
ass hour shit, and he's free of Luke the Fink with
his Washington up your ass connections, he's
being bad Rusty and it's years, man, he wants to
holler hallo for a grizzer any size big ass beast.

They go, putting on the miles, walking ten
yards apart, crossing bare ridgelines when they
feel they far enough away from Luke to take the
chance, then ducking back to timber when they
hear whirlybird Cop Turd glomming over the
next hill, yeah, Luke has put in a call, round up
those strays, shit, no one is going to round them
up. And after an hour, a good sweat on each,
father and son sweat, a little alike, a little diff,
Rusty got just a hint of sweet rot in his smell
but when the balls is back in as now he's okay,
many a hero smell worse than old Rust, and they
go like two combat wolves, eyes to the left, eyes
to the right, slow relaxed sweep, looking, listening to the *mood*, man, their steps keen off each
little start of sound, squirrels on a split ass, working upwind through the timber, skirting all the
alder, briers, snag-brush, working their way into
the wind as if they going to *smell* that bear. And
when they stop to rest, they are real good, man,
tight as combat buddies, they pick a spot under
an overhang rock at their back so no bear can
come up behind and the touch, just the feather

on your ass touch, of danger, cause grizzer could
be anywhere near, is ozone bubble in the nose,
that oo oo oo of the nose when you going to
meet a real hot fuck in an hour and you know
she there waiting for you, whoo-ee, whoo-ee,
humping a sweet pump by the railroad track
beautiful big-ass Texas night. Rusty starts to
talk. They looking out off a ledge onto a view
of stone ice peaks twenty miles away, could be
Colorado, not Alaska in September, and those
mountains full of evergreen dropping in long
fat sweet ass sweet husband fat-ass type of lines,
the rolling stands of evergreen looking like fur
on the ass of the grizzer, yeah, those soft humps
of mountains are like sleeping bears, big haunches
of hibernation, Hiram, and Rusty starts to point
out the local flora, the tall saxifrages like the
boykinia, the sowdock, fireweed, horsetail, he
been pointing them out all along as they were
going, just a quiet little voice, "That's white bell
of heather over there, D.J." or "Hot damn, look
at the height of those horsetails," "White mountain avens, boy, pretty flower that," "Purple
rhododendrons, up in the Circle! Wait till I tell
your mother I saw purple rhododendrons in the
Arctic Circle." Oh, there's cow parsnip and climbing bells, yellow arctic poppies, more of a fine

white little flower he calls saxifrage again. "Know what saxifrage means, kid?"

"You tell me."

"Rock buster. That little white flower is a rock buster. Any saxifrage is strong enough to grow and split a rock." And D.J. reels with that, cause he thinks of the little green shoot (or is it white? underground, just nipple tit out of the seed) getting its white nose into the smallest crack of the rock and pushing and the rock pushing back, and it swelling to crack the rock, and the rock not cracking, how can a soft shoot move rock? Yeah, well it sends out the word to the root and the root pulls into the basic ass power of the earth and draws a force, a subterranean thunder, Wanda, and womb, woom woom woom, one little blast of swell, that shoot is harder than rock for one micromillionth of a second, it got a hard on, Herbert, and the rock stone pussy cracks, and up comes boykinia the local saxifrage. Just rock buster. D.J. is humper-ding with sweet pores of thought. Damn.

"That's monkshood," says Rusty.

About then was when they first sat looking out across a canyon and a long field of tundra turning red and yellow already and a pioneer tree in the middle of it.

"Man, you like to be a tree by yourself in the middle of a field?" asks Rusty.

"Now you know I really don't know," says D.J. confessing ignorance for the first time since thirteen.

"My grandmammy, your great-grandmother Eula Spicer Jethroe, used to be a witch, so everbody claims. She used to tell me when I was a little three-year-old still shit ass in my breeches that I must never sleep under a pioneer tree, cause it is full of sorrow and alone and bats piss on it at midnight, therefore it stands by itself getting messages, all kind of special messages, and if you sleep under it, you witched by it, you get the messages too."

"What are they?"

"I don't know. Old Eula Spicer Jethroe wouldn't say." Yeah, they laughed. D.J. said, oh, cautious as they come, "Rusty . . . sir . . . how do you know the names of all this grass . . . herb . . . all this."

"Why I spent a half hour talking to Luke asking the names. That's the only good half hour I had with him. Cause that used to be my hobby. When I was your age I used to be a walking compendium of Texas wild flowers."

"Say, you never let on."

"Well, D.J., my daddy had more time, you

137

know. Him and me were close, you know cause
it was all that time, depression, East Texas depression years, cold heart times. He had no work
so we went hunting for meat. Then two years
later he hit a well and the Jethroes was rich
again, but those two years I saw sights, learned
things. We used to camp out in a lean-to right
on the plains. Coyotes. Oh, that's a cry."

"I've heard it hunting."

"Yeah, but in a lean-to set up so the rain don't
blow in the open end, and starting a fire in the
rain, know how to do that?"

"No, sir."

"Well, you got to look for a stump that's pro-
tected by overhang, or the underside of a tree
branch that's rotten, you got to find dry punk,
that dry perfumy sort of rot stuff in a tree, and
that's your tinder and your paper all in one. If
it's dry, it will get wet twigs to burn. So, that
we used to do, daddy and me, used to camp out
there four days in a row, trailing across that plain
till an animal got in range, not so easy when the
plain is bare, you hear, and we had to make the
shots count too, I learned a lot from my daddy,
he taught me one thing I'm going to teach you
now—the only time a good man with a good
rifle is in trouble is when he steps from sunlight

into shadow, cause there's two or three seconds when you can't see."

"I know that, daddy," says D.J.

"Yeah, but you never made a principle of it. That's the difference."

"Yessir, yessir."

"Listen, know the worst thing I ever saw. It was a poor deer being killed by an eagle. Some hunter had wounded the deer—the eagle finished the job or was about to when I couldn't stand to watch no more and shot the eagle and put the poor deer out of its miz. But that eagle had swooped in, plucked out one eye of the deer, fluttered up a little you know like a Nigger strutting his ass feathers, and then plucked the other eye. It was going to go for the nuts next. Terrible creature the eagle. I've heard they even pull the intestine out of a carcass like a sailor pulling rope with his mouth. It got me so upset to recognize that E Pluribus Unum is in the hands of an eagle that I almost wrote an open letter to the Congress of America. Can you imagine your daddy getting that ape shit? But I think it's a secret crime that America, which is the greatest nation ever lived, better read a lot of history to see how shit-and-sure a proposition that is, is nonetheless represented, indeed even symbolized by an eagle, the most miserable of the scavengers, worse than crow."

On and on they go for half an hour, talking so close that D.J. can even get familiar with Rusty's breath which is all right. It got a hint of middle-aged fatigue of twenty years of doing all the little things body did not want to do, that flat sour of the slightly used up, and there's a hint of garlic or onion, and tobacco, and twenty years of booze gives a little permanent rot to the odor coming off the lining of the stomach, and there's even a speck of caries, one bit of dental rot almost on the agreeable side (for face it, fellow Americans, there are secret freaked-out grope types who dig dental rot if its subtle kind of high clean funky smell, how often, after all, does a nose get near a living nerve?) but with all this detraction, fatigue, booze, Nick the Teen, garlic and cavity, it's still a good breath, it got muscle and a big happy man with that clean odorless white American flesh (hey assholes out there, is this D.J. addressing you a Texas youth for sure or is he a genius of a crippled Spade up in Harlem making all this shit up, better wonder, work your bronze, this is a problem—whose consciousness you getting, overlap on the frequencies, Percival? shit. D.J. is going to make you fly up your own ass before you get to read him

right, it's love to have the consciousness of D.J.,
Texas youth, better believe, cause it's easier for
D.J. to imitate a high I.Q. Harlem Nigger time
to time, since D.J. knows New York, yeah, he
passed through, MacDougal Street you wait and
see, than for a Harlem Nigger ever to know all
this secret Texas shit. Well, place your bets,
worry your head audience of D.J. there is no
security in this consciousness, and you are going
to die some day and there is no security in that,
well, before you buy your casket Mr. Rot Gut
wait till you get to know Tex and his own daddy
Gottfried Hyde Senior, the undertaker, there's
a piece of woo, and point coming here, point
your nose, auditor, is that D.J. riding on currents
of love can take all the smell of his daddy's
breath and love him still, cause that's love—you
can go to the end of the other's breath and still
forgive him. If you husbands and wives out
there in receiving land cannot do that, well,
hump your shrug, all is not hopeless, maybe you
still in love if only with limp dick and just one
lip of the pussy, or two lips of cunt dry as ad-
hesive tape. Woo-ee!) D.J. takes his consciousness and by act of will zooms with Superman
moves of his brain projectile back to ledge, back
to rock, and Rusty pointing across the valley to
a caribou upwind from them, a caribou just

standing near the pioneer tree, and Rusty lifts
his rifle, breathes, waits to feel D.J.'s mood, waits,
puts down his rifle. "Shall we let it go?"

"Yeah."

"Yeah, son. Shit, let's let old caribou go. He
suffering anyway."

And that old caribou is standing with his nose
in the moss, digging his nose in, and his haunches
are hicking and twitching and his stump tail is
wiggling like a baby's running nose. Alaska flies
are murdering him, he stands, suffers, then makes
a dash for two hundred yards to escape the flies,
stands, looks for damp in the tundra, holds it,
suffers the flies, then runs again, on up to the
ridge where there will be wind maybe, maybe
there will be wind, and he can clear his head
from thirty fly bite on the minute. And Rusty
and D.J. watching have been waiting for fifteen
minutes, and there's fine cool in them now, they're
off the fever of hunting and into the heart of it,
the cool, letting that caribou go has got them
so ready for bear they could believe in man-bear
radar, it's as if now they know, cause the pitch
of secret tune is pure that grizzer is near, something big is by. And as they step out, they have
not gone one-half of a mile before they find a
track, fresh bear track on the wet earth of a
high mountain rivulet, and their hearts hold,

cause track is big, Rusty could put the soles of
both his big hunting shoes inside that one bear's
foot, and mark of the claws in front is long, two
inches long of claws, this is grizzer, grizzer baby,
never black bear, not with claws two inches long.
Now they feel the size. They've been thinking
of grizzer as a big big man, about as frightening
as a stone-black seven-foot three-hundred-pound
Nigger, but grizzer is bigger than that, grizzer
is right up there with the hippopotami and the
small elephants, and the big elephants, yeah,
that's how it feels, now they feel alone and in
the woods with some fast dark boxcar size of
beast moving somewhere around in relation to
them. Shit! And the Cop Turd comes by overhead shaking the silence, and failing to see them
in the woods, and Rusty says in a hoarse little
clearing of his throat (just like a little clearing
in the forest) "Hey, now, D.J., we're on bear
traveling trail." And through the brush ahead is
a path, looks like it's been grooved by many a
grizzer working down the same route through
the brush, and there and here, bark rubbed from
trees, familiar intimate family rub of itching hide
and itching bear asshole rubbing against that
old corncob bark. Yeah, some nappy mountain
of grizzly has been lumbering and slinging his
legs along here. And D.J. breathes death—first

time in his life—and the sides of the trail slam
onto his heart like the jaws of a vise cause that
grizzer could come erupting out of the brush,
could a grizzer travel at speed through that
brush? it's death D.J.'s breathing, it comes like
attack of vertigo when stepping into dark and
smelling pig shit, that's what death smells to
him, own pig shit smell, terrible fear right out
of his lungs and pores, mucous lining of now
flappy-ass organs, and back of fear like man
riding chariot pulled by eight wild pigs in harness
is crazy-ass murder, cause D.J. for first time in
his life is hip to the hole of his center which is
slippery desire to turn his gun and blast a shot
into Rusty's fat fuck face, thump in his skull,
whawng! and whoong! with the dead-ass butt of
his Remington 721, D.J. is shivering on the
death in this hot-ass vale of breath, cause each
near-silent step of his toe on the tail sounds a
note, chimes of memory, angel's harp of ten
little toes picking out the blows of Rusty's belt
on his back, he five years old and shrieking off
the fuck of his head, cause the face of his father
is a madman ass, a power which wishes to beat
him to death—for what no longer known—a
child's screaming in the middle of, and so inter-
rupting, a Hallelujah Sir Jet Throne fuck? nobody know now, D.J. just remembers the beating,

screaming, pleading, smell of pig shit in his five-year-old pants, and death, coming in like oscillations red and green waves pulsating from oscilloscope, murder came red and green, stop, go, Rusty's eyes in to kill on D.J.—fat five-year-old spoiled beautiful little fuck in the middle between husband and wife, hola, Olatunji, vale of breath on the vise in his heart and first seed of tumor, figure-toi, could that be?—little pretty seed of backed-up murder passed from valve asshole Rusty's heart to the seat of D.J.'s brain, for Hallie rushed in then, picked up decanter whiskey, flung it through on a line through window, and glass crackled all scythe and lightnings, and spell broke, murder weather cracked in thunder, and D.J. all pig shit smell and five-year-old ass and back burning like the flesh in the burns of Hell run all screaming into Hallie's arms, little man saved by cunt, virility grew with a taint in the armature of the phallic catapult, call it tumor if that's what D.J.'s got in his brain, cause brilliance is next to murder, man, brilliance is green and gold light on the body and wings of horseflies hovering over the rot and gray-gold and red of degenerating meat. Whoo! Death is on him, memory of father near to murdering the son, breath of his own murder still running in the blood of his fingers, his hands, all murder

held back, and then on the trail came a presence,
no longer the fear of death but concentration,
murder between the two men came to rest, for
murder was outside them now, same murder
which had been beaming in to D.J. while he
thinking of murdering his father, the two men
turned to contemplate the beast. Which was
there? There before! No. Nothing to be seen. All
calm now, as if they walking into the flat ass
calm of a flat still sea, stepping in deeper on
every step, their bodies in different states of
immersion every breath, the late sun throwing
out orange-lavender, and lead of color near to
immersions now infusions of purple in deep of
the wood, and each step took them into different
domain, for D.J.'s nose was like a king surveying
the principalities of the realm, bleed you not,
Sigismunde, calm to calm they stepped on in
along the trail, each step a rock God laid on
water, hot horseshit Hercules, and hum the smells
in that wood, Prince of Pals, they took one step
through a kingdom of pines, mad genius pine
trees, prescribing their aromatic antiseptic pre-
scription for all things, incense saying come to
me I am all, I am siren of the North, nerve of
the Arctic Circle with affiliates down to the
Equator, I'm a brain, man, pine needles my
calling card.

Next step, in they're plunged into some rot, some stump of dwarf birch, bark rubbed ass of raw by tail of bear or moose of caribou antlers eight years ago! like that! and dying over the years, cause a ring of bark had been cut and the skin of such dying tree go to rot beneath the trunk, fell down. Into the open mouth of that remaining stump came the years of snow, sun, little jewels of bird shit, cries of sap from the long dying roots, the monomaniacal electric yodeling of insects, and wood rotting into rotting wood, into gestures of wood, into powder and punk all wet and stinking with fracture between earth and sky, yeah, D.J. could smell the break, gangrene in the wood, electric rot cleaner than meat and sick shit smell and red-hot blood of your flesh in putrefaction, but a confirmed wood gangrene nonetheless, Burbank, a chaos of odor on the banks of the wound, nothing smells worse than half-life, life which has no life but don't know it—thank you, Mr. Philosopher, just show me the hemorrhoids of the academy, and on that rock! . . . Next step was into a pool of odor which came from the sweets of the earth, sweet earth smell speaking of endless noncontempla-tive powers, beds of rest, burgeonings, spring of life, a nectar for the man's muscles on the odor of that breath, yeah, D.J. was breathing his last,

he was in the vale of breath, every small smell
counted, it was the most fucking delicious moment of his life up to that point, for there are
those who know and those who do not know
when a very bad grizz is near to you (a final
division of humanity) and D.J. knew, and D.J.
was in love with himself because he did not wish
to scream or plead, he just wished to encounter
Mr. D., big-ass grizz, and the next step put his
nose into an aisle of forest scents, herbs offering
each their high priest of here, here is the secret
lore and the cold fires of the temple, and leaf
mold, wet molderings, some kind of forest good-
bye weeded in from the messages of the wind,
sending back to the peasant, back to the farm,
then moss, new greenings, the odor of forest
beginnings like baby ass powder and tiny flowers,
the tenderness of the tip where life began, and
some sweet wine of old funk in the moss as well,
some odor of dwarf's armpits wiped with velvet,
thank you, milady.

That was when the griz came.

Around a turn in the trail, by the side of a
ledge, he'd been waiting, listening to the tick
snap and twig crack of their boots, and he came
at them from thirty yards away with the roar of
nothing D.J. ever heard, like a foghorn fire siren
about to burst, cause some congested hell in a

whirlwind has come thundering with rocks down a hill out of its foghorn throat and D.J. heard the crazy wild ass moan of every animal they'd gunned down and the tear and blast of all flesh from all fat exploded knockout Magnums, what a cry came out of that shit ass beast, and frozen like prisoners in the searchlight, hypnotized half up to sky, and the air shivered as if a .105 howitzer just gone off, the grizzer came at them on the heuuuuuu of the cry, two red coal little eyes of fire, wall of fur coming fast as a locomotive barreling on that trail, and D.J. in some sweet cool of rest below all panic and paralysis dropped to one knee, threw up Remington, had a sail of light at the top of his head of far-gone tree and sky, and pulled off the trigger to smash a shot into that wall of fur, almost leisurely, like shot-putting a rock into a barrel, his eye not even to the scope, you could not miss if your arm had the strength to get the gun up. And Rusty fired from behind and that animal didn't stop, it kept coming on down like a twelve-foot surf of comber bamming right for your head, and D.J.'s heart and his soul sweet angel bird went up the elevator of his body and all balls but flew out before he slammed bolt and fired again at grizzer not ten yards away flame of the muzzle meeting flame from grizzer's red flame ass red mouth, grizzer kerwhonked half in air from the blast, took leap, hop, howl, one mad bound off trail, leaving a wake of hot caves, gamy earth, fur went by so near, yeah, one flash of blood on his honey hide, and then he went booming down the mean crazy slope of the ledge, twisting D.J.'s neck, so fast was the move. Then grizzer was gone.

Well, now they had a pretty, didn't they? How sweet seemed Big Luke's precaution stay in open with the bear. Now they had to climb down that fucking ledge and somewhere down, down there in all that thicket and brush and owl shit slunk and precipitous slope was Mr. D., the Red Ball Express, half-dead or not nearly dead at all, awful bad. They are doing their best not to chatter, cackle, or carry on like birdwomen now. "Never heard of a grizzer charging like that," said Rusty's voice, weak as piss over pebbles.

"They gone ape shit just as Big Luke say." Hoarse adolescent big phlegm voice.

"Yeah." Humps.

"Yeah." Humps. Echo in the silences.

"I wish I had my Ruger right now," said Rusty, big-ass State Trooper style. "A rifle's too slow for tight-ass quarters."

"Was you going to bring it?"

"I almost took it up from Ding Bat today."

The Ruger 44 Magnum is Rusty's twelve-inch barrel pistol, detachable stock, comes highly recommended for bear in the brush. "That fucking Luke," says Rusty, "sticking us around the chimney—who's to know we'd end up here?"

They are waiting for the other to be first to say, "Let us go back to camp and come out tomorrow with the Ruger and the mob." But they can't, and the moment they are silent, echo of the event opens silence after silence—they are close to puking they are so scared. D.J. feels shit yellow between his toes, his bowels slosh internal bilge, every bit of hard shit in him has broken down to squirts like spit and dishwater rumblings. A pall is on the woods. He can smell nothing but randy ammonia in his armpits. Yeah. And like lightning which cut across the sleeper's bed so close that sleeper was turned and flung to the floor, so the memory of Mr. D. (D for Death) Grizzer's mad-ball charge is like a stroke across the strings of nerve in his life—say, it will come back and back again.

Yeah, recollected in memory, it comes back to D.J. eating in the Dallas ass manse, and he shivers—no man cell in him can now forget that if the center of things is insane, it is insane with force, heuuuuuu goes the bellow of the grizzer in the salt on his meat and sorrow. But bearable.

Cause they went down for the grizzer after all—
here is how—58% of D.J. wanted nothing but to
leave Mr. Wounded Grizzer and get the fuck
out, in fact that 58% was pulling on his liver and
gut. But D.J. is a head man. Which is not to say
he gives head, but is ruled by his head. A creature of will. That will now says to sixteen-year-
old flesh, "Go back without looking for this griz
and Tex will ride your ass to shit."

That's it. D.J. face the anger of God before he
look into the contempt and contumely of that
State of Texas personified by Gottfried Tex
Hyde Jr. Whooee.

"Well, dad, let's start down after the animal."

"Right, son," and Rusty smiles with lips like
two wet soda crackers flapping at each other.

And the grizz is there. Forty shit-eating minutes later, their back wet, legs trembling like
horse just run the mile and a quarter, their hands
slippery with coward oil (clam juice and sweat,
you bird watcher) faces scratched like two
bitches been working them over with *long* nails,
lad, rifle stocks scratched, their knees, thighs,
ribs and butts a congregate of bruises (which
congregate is the established plural for bruises,
look it up, turd pedant) their lungs fired from
fear, funk, exhaustion and the anticipation that
each step could back them into a wound-ass

grizzer, they worked their collective father and son ass down the steep slope below the edge, farting through catbrier brush, dwarf alder brush, blueberry cranberry brush, rocks, slick-ass rocks, sharp-ass rocks to cut their hands, ghost trees with roots half-exposed on the near precipices of the slope, trees taking on witches' arms for shapes, limbs beseeching the North—O, power above the Circle, incantations and greetings from this witches' tree.

Well, they went down one at a time following a trail of blood as thick and clean as Sherwin-Williams Red. D.J. would go first and Randy would cover him—combat men flushing out a sniper. Then Randy would make his trip and pass D.J., D.J. meanwhile scanning about him in a 360 degree circle which meant thirty feet of visibility here, one hundred there, and wonder. Cause the blood led down and down, as if Mr. D., his insides a rocket of exploded works, was plunging like a cannonball to the bottom of something, and yet. All grizzers crazy. What if Mr. D. went down and then circled up to take them from behind? So D.J. scanned three hundred and sixty degrees about, waited till Rusty beckoned from below and then started his scratch-ass descent on the trail of the griz, passing Rusty with the high hard sobs of lungs working too hard, and Rusty sobbing back. What a fucking dual coward-ass twin sweat and sob that was. Wham! That Texas will carries Texas cowards to places they never dreamed of being. Vava, va va voom!

After forty minutes they made rendezvous. The griz was lying in a beat-down circle of brush which he must have tromped out forty or fifty times while going through one of the bends of his wounds, and he had set down like a tabby cat on its stomach, forelegs tucked under him, peaceful, looking to be stuffed bear served on a red plate ten feet in diameter, for that blood beneath was monumental in its pool. They came on him from a hundred feet above, and Rusty was for pouring in some lead just to make shit-and-sure, but peace was coming off that bear— it was like the moment a gull sets on water— and so Rusty contented himself—being a camera-conscious flash-bulb poking American—to heist a little stone and bap that bear on the hide. Old Griz raised its head a little. Not dead yet. And its mouth looked to laugh as if between the mill-stones of two huge pains (or was it three huge gears from three huge wounds?) something very funny has occurred, as if he was saying, "You put your palm sweat on that stone, mother-fucker, and I'm taking your sweat with me."

Rusty raised his gun, but D.J. touched the rifle slightly with a little salute, and started walking down toward the bear.

"Come back," Rusty whispered, "you're out of your fucking head," for D.J. was holding his rifle in one hand swinging down around his thigh. "You cover me, daddy," said D.J. to avoid a fishwife family gone-for-gooney while that poor huge beast was going. D.J. just had to see him up close.

At twenty feet away, D.J.'s little cool began to evaporate. Yeah, that beast was huge and then huge again, and he was still alive—his eyes looked right at D.J.'s like wise old gorilla eyes, and then they turned gold brown and red like the sky seen through a ruby crystal ball, eyes were transparent, and D.J. looked in from his twenty feet away and took a step and took another step and another step and something in that grizzer's eyes locked into his, a message, fellow, an intelligence of something very fine and very far away, just about as intelligent and wicked and merry as any sharp light D.J. had ever seen in any Texan's eyes any time (or overseas around the world) those eyes were telling him something, singeing him, branding some part of D.J.'s future, and then the reflection of a shattering message from the shattered internal organs of that bear came

twisting through his eyes in a gale of pain, and
the head went up, and the bear now too weak
to stand up, the jaws worked the pain.

Then the gale subsided. The peace came back
to the eye, pain fading like the echo of the last
good note, and that wild wicked little look of
intelligence in the eye, saying something like,
"Baby, you haven't begun," and when D.J.
smiled, the eyes reacted, they shifted, they looked
like they were about to slide off the last face of
this presence, they looked to be drawing in the
peace of the forest preserved for all animals as
they die, the unspoken cool on tap in the veins
of every tree, yes, griz was drawing in some
music of the unheard burial march, and Rusty—
wetting his pants, doubtless, from the excessive
tension—chose that moment to shoot, and griz
went up to death in one last paroxysm, legs
thrashing, brain exploding from new galvaniz-
ings and overloadings of massive damage report,
and one last final heuuuuuu, all forgiveness gone.
And coughed blood out of his throat as he died.

D.J. didn't speak to Rusty on the way back.
And when they hit camp at dark, Big Luke so
relieved he couldn't even read various prescribed
riot acts, they asked at last who had got the bear,
and D.J., in the silence which followed, said,
"Well, we both sent shots home, but I reckon

Rusty got it," and Rusty didn't contradict him—one more long silence—and Rusty said, "Yeah, I guess it's mine, but one of its sweet legs belongs to D.J." Whew. Final end of love of one son for one father.

Next morning, crack ass of dawn, Rusty was overseeing the transfer of that dead and now dressed grizzer from his dried blood patch up the winch to the helicopter. And they figured the bear in his natural state had stood nine hundred pounds and more counting the claws.

★

INTRO BEEP 9

★

The hunting over? This fine narrative of native Texas pluck and grits now to be laid back into its rifle case while D.J.'s mind opens up another box of strict inside goodies? Screw. The climax within Alaska is yet to come—you will get rocks off you thought were buried forever. But rest for an inst. Return to civ, which is to say syphilization and fuck James Joyce—now enter D.J.'s genius head working its ventral hatch and vale, which is to say his *mouth*, turd nugget! at the dinner cited before in the Dallas ass manse, D.J. eighteen, two years later, composing in his head (while smiling at Texas tooth and cunt hostess

158

types to right and left of him)—reach for your brains, Mr. Intellectual Testicles—let us snap down deep into D.J.'s mind patterns, and see if we pick up a universal mandolin or two, spelled mandala, dear Major Galliana, frostbite and fuck hairs, there is no logic to projects but incest, family bugger—you want to see D.J. the brain? he is working out the secret inner logic of piss. Now D.J. is a shit-oriented late adolescent, he is marooned, in case you have not noticed, on that balmy tropical isle pronounced Selador, spelled cellardoor—asshole—do you know a committee of Language Hump-type professors put out a committee finding back in 1936—most beautiful word in the English language is cellardoor. Think of that. The Isle of Selador—think of that. The Isle of Selador—otherwise known as cellardoor, the entrance to your asshole. Where we began was with fact one—D.J. is marooned on the balmy tropical isle of Anal Referent Metaphor. Now that's a moniker, man. You can see the fellow stand up and walk around, Anal Referent Metaphor! He's confidential secretary to America's #1 financial wizard Mr. Isower Anal Compulsive. You can write a fucking play suitable for staged readings about the confidential dialogue between the two. As viz:

Isower Anal Compulsive—How was your movement, today, Referent Metaphor?

Anal Referent Metaphor—Loose and slicky ass, Isower. How was yours?

I.A.C.—Bonded. We got to move some capital down the list.

A.R.M.—Set up a technical slide?

I.A.C.—For shit-and-sure, Señor Manure.

That's how they talk in the East, up in those bone Yankee ass Jew circumcised prick Wall Street palaces—take it from D.J.—he got psychic transistors in his ear (one more gift of the dying griz) which wingding on all-out pickup each set of transcontinental dialogues from the hearts of the prissy-assed and the prigged. Fungatz, radatz, and back to piss.

What can D.J. have to say about piss which is new? Whoo whoo. Piss, pious pretender, is a nerve of the wind when it's drilled from a peter. Rushings of the air, balms of the limbs (which is what air is, sexy). Piss, fascinated auditor of D.J.'s intellectual shuttlings and switchings, is a lullaby of the waters when it poozles from a damp pussy. So get your turns recorded. Problem of piss broken down into two. Peter piss and cunt piss. Phallic urine, Vaginal urine. You're dealing with different details, Delilah, P.U. and V.U.

Well this is deep stuff. Excrement is defeat.
Liquid excrement otherwise known as You're-In
Spa-ce-man is the defeat which comes from
stand-up ventures where you had to wait. Some-
one talking, and you want to interrupt but you
hold your tongue—that makes for piss. Gather
near, D.J. tell you why. An impulse once it is
frustrated' crystallizes the chemicals which had
been interacting in order to fuel the move. Why?
Say, son, take something on faith. D.J. genius
philosopher and commo engineer (that's communications, not Come-you-nism, Senator, although it's a mistake any intelligent Southerner
might make) D.J., Grand Synthesizer of the
Modern Void, suggests that the intellectual
equipment to comprehend why frustration makes
crystals of impulse when they are in the mode of
liquid chemical matter is not yet yours. Study
basic electricity, basic electronics. Come back.
D.J. will stick an electrode up your ass. Now
consider, take it on faith: a crystal is a receiving
apparatus to draw in messages, because it's a
form, man, a crystal is the most acute kind of
form and forms are receptors of that which is
less formed because that which is less formed
looks to define itself by getting fucked by a
form. You hip? That's why beauty stands still
and lets a piece of ass come to it. Cause beauty

is a high form. It is a crystal. It is the frustrated
impulse of a general desire to improve the creation. So it fixed, man. How else comprehend the
flowers? They get all the messages. Ever heard of
a flower coming to you? Only its scent. But avoid
complexities and reversals of direction at this
stage—do not try to solve positive and negative
electricity, rather gather on D.J.'s observed fact:
frustration makes you telepathic, cause the cat's
whisker (which is the frustrated nerve still dan-
gling from the residue of the frustration) tickles
that new-formed crystal of the impulse till the
electronic message comes in. Frustration makes
you more telepathic because it makes you more
electric. Up to a point, Poindexter, after that,
dielectric, apathetic, insulated, you ass. Cause
to be telepathic while frustrated is to be burned
on charged wire. After the bomb comes apathy.
So call for the flushing waters. Your body, D.J.
would inform you, sends out a call to all cell
waters: gather here, kiss this crystal, dissolve its
form. Unloose my stasis. Crystal washes down to
glub, glub, glub. Urine is a pipe running the
dissolution of all unheard messages. That's why
people piss like horses at good parties and bad—
they are getting uncouth oceanic messages from
all over the room: come here, I want to fuck you;
go there, I want to kill you. Whoo-ee! That blad-

der gets full of piss. Therefore, D.J. seeks to avoid all frustration of impulse in order to test his hypothesis. For figure thee, Henry, if D.J. makes it through a day without a single impulse held back, he should not need to piss a drop. That's science, dear clients.

CHAP NINE

At the party in Dallas ass manse, D.J. and Tex have each lined up the possible tooth and cunt hostesses they can fuck. That is simple. Some tooth and cunt hostesses are closet fucks. Walk in on them in an unlocked bathroom and you can have a two minute red-hot steaming ass blubber wet slap-dizzy oceanic cunt fuck. Need never fuck them again, understood, or don't fuck them again for six months. You just taking two minutes out of the tissue of responsible executive country club station wagon et cetera shit et cetera shit life. Key to it all, cause not all do, is don't make a mistake, adolescents! with the wrong kind of tooth and cunt responsible hostess type or she'll kick your nuts in: you got to pick the one with the right schizophrenia, that beam in the eye, that gleam of the mind which says I keep a closet for occasions, meet you on the moon for a sixty-second suck. Well, when fucking these mad insane ones, D.J. here to advise, get in fast, get out fast, cause they greedy fiends. This ain't young cunt from which you cop the goods—this is used cunt, burnt meat, cliff-hanging menopause types which can't get rid of the poisons by any hole but the pussy hole. They greedy fucking fiends. You accept their invitation on leaving the bathroom to make it with them in a motel and they get more out of you in three hours than a new chick emanating happy fucks would elicit in a day and a night. And the tooth and cunters are converting their schizophrenia into cancer juice for you. This too deep and disagreeable? Listen, loves, we getting back to Alaska soon, but Tex and D.J. for present period in their eighteen- and nineteen-year-old life are super-hot business cause they got illicits going, nobody like Tex and D.J., wait'll you hear.

They also on freak activities. Not just fucking two or three forty-year-old women on separate shots in the bathroom in one night, after all that's nothing once you read the Marquis de Sade, but

they off on real freaks. For instance, they are
digging corpses in Tex's father's funeral parlor,
I don't mean the ultimate, the boys are never
without some kind of jammed-up taste and
principles but listen city slickers from the East,
they are engaging in private autopsies, under-
cover undertaker surgical activities—this weird
unpalatable action to be explained on the basis
that it gives them powers. They are not hunter-
fighter-fuckers for nothing, no, nor with en-
claves of high ability in karate, football, sports
car, motorcycle, surfboard, and certain notions
of the dance, as well as genius inquiries in electronics and applied existentialism without having
to snoop here and there for powers, which they
get from crime, closet fucking, potential over-
turn of incest since Tex is almost not above trying to get Hallie Jethroe in one closet fuck this
very night, plus ghoul surgery on corpses which
is demonological you may be shit-and-sure, and
derives from their encounter with all the human
shit and natural depth of their Moe Henry hunt
two years ago.

So back to Alaska where the boys got their
powers. And they got them all Alaska style, as
weird and wild-ass as the entrails of a wild-ass
goose, just listen to this: D.J. was in such a
murder ball of sick disgusted piss-on-dad after

Rusty took claim of the bear that he couldn't
sleep for fear he'd somnambulate long enough
to beat in Rusty's head, so up he got, tapped Tex
in his bunk, wide-awake as well, and in one
whispered minute they decided to split and make
a little trek right that night into Endicott Range.
And that's where they are now (in D.J.'s mind
two years later) right out in those hills eight
miles already from Dolly Ding Bat, packboards
carrying tent-cloths, grub, rifles, blankets, man
they made their packs in the dark without wak-
ing Big Luke, Al Bell, Ollie, Rusty, or the medium
assholes (who are all sleeping sound as slaughtered cattle) and off they go, taking the trail up
the mountain, staying to the trail till dawn which
is like four in the morning this part of September
after the long Arctic twilight night of June and
July and the very short night of August, so now
the weather getting ready to take the dip into
winter, they are working on the last of the early
dawns.

It's hours before they speak, just working along
in the early fall nip cold of the August night,
breathing in hint of the chill of the frozen steam
and the icy vise of magnetic north—all those cold
gun blue compass needles pointing to you magnetic North—how cold can you take it? a problem which D.J. Goethe Rousseau James Clerk

Max'ell pot n acid head all rolled into one Dallas T formation high school ass is going to prong into in the future or even right now—I mean do you have hard-on enough fraternity stud fucker Lambda Lambda Omicron Mu jockstrap frathouse faggot to put your red-hot daddy-loved-you ding into a cake of ice? Shit you do, Señor Shinola. Ice even numbs King Kong's dong. And all the needles point to the North where the icy Pole *is*—dig, node hunter? That tip which catches all the electromagnetic focus and funnel of that electromagnetic field called earth by the common clay (otherwise known as U.S. finger fuck voter) is exactly the place where the ice is, and that ice is the orifice, now you're cooking, cutey, that's to where the field runs, nay *flows* out from the center of the earth to go around the earth into the other end (South Pole, Newton!) and back through the fires, the molten red lava flaming shit furnace at the core where the heat is, changing all the way over to ice again as the electromagnetic field and steam passes from inside blazes to outside crust, and that deep cold on the crust node pole is the Encyclopedia of Cataclysmic Knowledge all refined down in the spooky early morning chill of Alaska August night up above the Circle, man, there're not ghosts up there, but communes of spookiness, pales, dominions, psycho swingers—even telepathies, Euripides, Alaska above the Circle is something else, and not just Aurora Borealis (which is also something else)—listen, dear limpidity of the intelligent ear which has cashed in its wax for hand-in-hand progression through these conceptual coils with D.J., we are going back to Aurora Borealis cause it is the only mountain of heavenly light which is certified to be result and product of magnetic disturbances—dig! you long patient asshole, we are on the track of something—that early morning chill is tuning the boys up because they getting the stone ice telepathic hollow from the bowels of the earth after it passed through the magnetic North Pole orifice. (Say now what's the dif between earth and flesh? Earth orifice is ice, whereas flesh orifice? have you check out your bunghole fever reading lately? Think about that, all you concept-bound Yankee dry suck minds, y'need a little Texas oil in the pan, in the brainpan, Samantha.) That indeed is why Texas soil is so poor grit dry—all the goodness is down in that oil, all that fever and fuck lust percolating beneath. "Man," says Tex (after four hours' silence) "it was about time we did our split ass from that hunk shit safari." Tex, D.J. is here to tell you, has what they call a cold mien. Yeah, a real cold mean. He's a killer, baby,

got one of those dull Texas faces to prove it. It's
when he look interested and happy that you got
to watch out, cause like the poet said, somebody
is going to be dead. In fact, Tex is a looker, like
D.J. He's tall, got a whippy old body, 6-1, 168
pound, all whip leather, saber and hide even
when he seventeen. He and D.J. are lookalikes,
except for expression, cause D.J. is full of mother-
love received in full crazy bitch perfume aromas
from Hallie, whereas Tex is full of ape shit daddy-
love. Gottfried Hyde Senior, the fattest strongest
fuck of an undertaker in Dallas ass County, had
four girls in one marriage and then a fifth in the
other (first wife died and he buried her with the
services of his own mortician parlor—some under-
takers got no shame) and second wife, the stringy
Texas girl from fifty-two Texas shacks backs
right to the Alamo got it up to give him a son
on the second installment to emerge from her
honest hardworking womb and snatch. She had
a real pick and pull of a pussy, D.J. always
divined, just a mean skinny Texas snapper, a
lobster claw of a cunt, just the type to turn on
a fat bull of a Gottfried Hyde cause he looked
to be one of those massive men with a little
peeny dick, who, reason suggests, like a pussy
which is quick, rubbery, pinchy as a thumb and
finger—what else you going to get out of a short

dick but a preference for girls who got the tunnel muscle at the front tip? This study of cunnubial arts by D.J. is grand hypothetical, cause D.J., owning God's blessing, is well hung, in fact he has a dick like a Nigger, but for hue, Renfrew, and it's one place he got it slightly over Tex—the Measure Your Dick Department. Anyhoo (cry if you got a short dick) Gottfried Hyde was torralee and cockaloo over his son Gott Hyde Junior, and raised him with the blessing of full love till he was five or six and developed a mind of his own, but no more of that unless we can take a visit to the back rooms at the embalmers, which, being our scene set only in Alaska and Dallas ass manse, we therefore cannot. But, full of daddy-love, Tex got that mean glint in the eye for which Texans are justly proud and famous, whereas D.J. has got the sweet smile of my-momma-loved-me-and-I'm-sweet-as-a-birthday-cake kind of mean look, you know like where the hell is it coming from next? As a team, by any reckoning, they're superbas, can't stop them, they a natural hunting couple. And now that it's morning, they stop, cook a little breakfast, figuring the smoke will be broken by the trees in the wood in which they cook so that Cop Turd won't spot their fire. Besides it's too early. They'll assume at Ding Bat the boys are off for a pre-breakfast hike. They do not yet know that the boys is off on a bona fide tear. Cause what they see is a range of mountains ahead with real peaks, and they are going to go on up into them. (Ice needle peaks are crystals to capture the messages of the world.)

There! You all posed y'all ready for the next adventure in the heartland of the North, well hold your piss, Sis, we're about to embark with Tex Hyde who is, insist upon it, a most peculiar blendaroon of humanity and evil, technological know-how, pure savagery, sweet aching secret American youth, and sheer downright meanness as well as genius instincts for occult power (he's just the type to whip asses at the Black Masses) as well as being crack athlete. Such consummate bundle of high contradictions talks naturally in a flat mean ass little voice. Better hear it.

Moreover, take a turn, pigeons, wheel on a bird whistle, D.J. is calling you back to look at Gottfried Hyde Senior and his second wife Jane McCabe Hyde, mother of you know which Tex. Now Gottfried Senior, nickname Gotsie or Gutsy, is in his element when up to the elbows in intestinal slime or a bull fuck. He's bull fuck faggot fucker (pederast, you ass) bull fuck sheep fucker, bull fuck waitress fucker, he'd even fuck a keyhole if it was the size appropriate to a castle door. (There's aisles and vales in that cold metallic chamber lock.) Gutsy will fuck any orifice, nostril, ear, asshole, mouth or any crevice, navel, even cream between two fat tits (that's a 'tweener fuck) he'll rub your armpit off, he'll split the crack in your athlete's foot, there's no telling what legion of prongings and proctorings has been delivered to the boxcar of corpses which pass through the marble hall of Mortuary Manor. Now D.J. ain't lost his sense of exquisite impeccable taste. He's not bullshitting you one bit— Gutsy calls his humming thriving corpse stuffer establishment nothing other than G. Hyde's Mortuary Manor, which of course all the Dallasassians have promptly broken down to Gutsy's Double M Kasket Klub. First question to ask yourself is Gutsy such a champion prong sadist bull fuck because he is an undertaker, or did he come into being an undertaker because he is a prong fucker first? Either way, chicken or egg, leave him loose with a cow, a horse (preferably mare—not even Gutsy 5-11, 280 pounds of human living bull can stick it up a stallion's ass) leave Gutsy with a jackass, a goat, a poor little old dog, or a plumb piece of human pudding too appetizing to be called a corpse, for the Ghost has but departed, give Gutsy a purchase on any hint of cave, tunnel, scratch, or groove, and he will take his peeny dick and lather up a storm. He even jacks off twice a day. W'nston Churchill used to drink a bottle of brandy and smoke twenty cigars dai'v until he was eighty more and dead. Gutsy Hyde jacks off twice a night and will until he's nine*v. But he's no freaked-out onanist—that's just excess froth. Gutsy has come an average of eight to ten times a day, seven days a week for forty plus years. The unknown statistic in the whole State of Texas, the secret spring to the coils and crazy fucked-up clockwork of Tex, D.J.'s ace, Tex Hyde, is simply that his daddy comes more often than anyone in the whole fuc'ing state from cowpuncher to President and back again. And how does D.J. know all this? Well, everybody in Dallas who has ever come within hailing distance of Gutsy Hyde has felt the bull advancement of his persona. I mean, he grope you silly. You get caught in a corridor with G.H., Gott in Himmel, protect your parts, Gutsy will start to breathe heavy, he put his arm around you, he rub next to you, if you good and strong, and shove him off, or slipperywise and slip away, he's come already, just that contact cloth to cloth, his pin in a crease of his pants, he's hot nuts, he's a Texas gusher. Gutsy comes all over the place out of a vast enthusiasm for life (or

some such disease of unbalance as the fucked-
out cynics would say) no, Gutsy present a problem, what can make a man come so thumping
much, and the answer is—D.J. whispers it—
corpsemanship. Gutsy is tuned in to the Pha-
raoh's art, he's a libido hunter, a human dredge,
dragging bottoms and pissing out bilge through
that peeny dick of his, while consuming all aura
and effluvia of libido. Gutsy is always catching
and clutching a hair of the wetstone in his fat
fuck greedy fingers or is equally gusto at bur-
rowing away at the warmth, sweet, love, and
fuck sugar of the universe inasmuch as these gifts
of sunshine and generation are deployed, scat-
tered, and distributed through men, women,
dogs, goats, here we go again.

Now, Tex' ma, Jane McCabe Hyde, is on the
side of being a saint. She cooks, cleans, mends,
worries, does without a servant until pushed to
the point of necessity, takes no time to herself,
works for all, never grumbles, has the sunlight of
the sea in the glint of her cornea, and in fact
she'd qualify for Texas ass saint, female division,
except for her pussy, that thumb and finger
grip of real live snapper. Ever see a Southern
Methodist halfback knife a line like a catapult
had sprung him through, well, that's the Literary

Handbook Metaphor Manual for old Jane Mc-
Cabe Hyde and her secret pussy which keeps
her from saint category. And how does D.J. know
about this secret beautiful snap spring of pussy,
well, Gottfried Hyde has told everyone in town
about the wonders of his second wife's cunt,
he has wanted people to know why he married
her since she was then poor, unknown, plain of
face, whereas Gutsy had married up first crack
out, had got into some Country Club money shit,
enough to set up his first Kasket Klub from which
Mortal Man or Double M emerged. Yeah. So he
didn't want on the death of his first wife (whom
some would insinuate was fucked to death, although after bearing four girls, others could sug-
gest that her maternal flappy-lip old rubber box
was so big, Gottfried could have put his two
meat-trust hands around his peeny dick in prayer
and still got in) but dying from too much or too
little off Gutsy's peeny old prick, Mr. Hyde the
undertaker did not want, once his first rich
beauty was gone, for people to think he was
taking a single step down. So he bragged up a
storm about the glories of Jane's Secret Sleeper
until some were even curious to get in for them-
self, although offered no chance. Jane had the
blessing of the Alamo in her. All that secret

springiness been passed down in the seed, boy, anybody in the direct line of the heroes of the Alamo got seed like Mexican jumping beans, cause when all those Alamo troopers maintained to their positions and didn't piss in no pants and held their shit, tight honorable asshole in the face of certain death, and hung on, why a cloud and vale of love rose up about them in the middle of all this Mexican fire and shit storm, they was all loving their buddies so much, cause, man, they was the best bunch of sinewy high bounding zap and God streak fuckers, and each time one of them got one of Santa Ana's rounds in his virile little old Alamo heart, why, the fuck went up to death with a spring of joy, cause his buddies and his far-gone relatives (from whom the poor trooper hadn't had a letter in a year) were going to be nonetheless spiritual beneficiaries, and the spiritual essence of secret zinging semen went across the desert and through the air on the trooper's last breath and gave swinger pricks and springing cunts to some of the best and worst people in Texas. (Which accounts for why it's such a crazy state.) Yeah, go back to the martyrs of the Alamo, and add a picture of Tex and his parents, Gutsy and Jane, in cameo, and you get a notion of the kink which resides in the heart of the Lone Star. Now, carry on up to the mountains where soon . . . patience, patience, dear poontang, why it's on patience and poontang that they built the West. We can always get to the boys.

★

INTRO BEEP 10

★

Yeah, the boys is up in the boreal-montane coniferous forest biome (dig! shit ecologist big university librarian groper) and that biome may run from Labrador to western Alaska, but it about ready to give out, it's had it, all that three-to four-thousand-mile patch of balsam fir and black spruce, piss on that, wolverines, we ain't seeing much more of the tamarack on the stream sides, and the willows, the birch, the alder and the poplars (all concealing their Doppler effect, Wolfgang!) no, the boys are stepping up the south slopes of the foothills of the Brooks Range and those mountains ahead, forget it, that's where the real church of the spirits goes congregating in cathedrals of black ice, blue ice, white snow, land of the dream spirits, listen asshole America, D.J. your disc jockey is telling you, where you going when you sleep? well, hole, there's only one place you go, and that's into the undiscovered magnetic-electro fief of the dream, which is opposed to the electromagnetic field of the earth just as properly as the square root of minus one is opposed to one. Right! They never figured out yet whether light is wave, corpuscle, or hung up on finding her own identity, all they know once you get down to it is that light is bright, and therefore not necessarily opposed to being part of Universal Mind, henceforth known as UM which is the fat frog you calling for, Volta, when you clear your throat (um) and look for inspiration (um). Cough up an oyster, roll that phlegm, diddle it around your finger, Clem—you can't get fucked for less—here is the sweet intimate underground poop: when you go into sleep, that mind of yours leaps, stirs, and sifts itself into the Magnetic-Electro fief of the dream, hereafter known as M.E. or M.E.F., you are a part of the spook flux of the night like an iron filing in the E.M. field (otherwise glommed as e.m.f.) and it

all flows, mind and asshole, anode and cathode,
you sending messages and receiving all through
the night, if you had your nose in garlic and
been bum fucking the wrong cunt, well the route
this yere night is through the dreams of the
witches, that's a circuit, Perkins, lots of shit, and
if you clean as milk and had your nose all day
up the antiseptic asshole of Big H the Corporate
Hospital Corporation, why then your dreams got
to go through the incinerator where they pile all
the old hospital bandages, all that dried blood
pus shit green gangrene bladder gut mess—that's
a battery—from all the surgery of the day which
surgery had duly excised and thereby assassi-
nated one hundred plus organs from seventy-
eight patients, a confusion in the Divine Economy, as all those organs taking millions of years
to make (think of the evolution of the cells) are
now being flushed in a gush into the incinerator
while the surgeons get their clean whiskey-free
libidinal juice—I mean, man, just think of being
able to knife somebody and get paid for it—any-
how, Mr. Clean Milk, with your nose up Corporation's antiseptic asshole, it seems by this itin-
erary that your dreamland route, your M.E.F.
trip ticket, your private sleep circuit goes right
through that incinerator bag in the hospital gut
pile, dream on that, all your messages all going

through those amputated organs, ugh, all the Bunnies dreaming of nunneries, no matter what
route, if the message go from you across the bed
to your dear mate (rot in your own breath,
spoiler mine) or if you flinging a thought all the
way from Dallas to Alaska and back again, just
no chance, know this, you a part of the dream
field, you the square root of minus one, you off
in a flux, part of a circuit, you swinging on the
inside of the deep mystery which is whatever is
electricity, and who is magnetism? for they the
in and out, the potential and actual, the about
to be and the becoming of Something—we cannot call it love, the lust of Satan, can that be?
Magnetism potential and electricity the actual of
the Prince himself? whoo-ee, say D.J., cause his
genius brain can grope ultimates and that's not
for every short-hair butterball in town, no, figure
this, the electricity and magnetism of the dream
fief is reversed—God or the Devil takes over in
sleep—what simpler explanation you got, M.A.
expert type? nothing better to do than put down
Mani the Manichee, well, shit on that, D.J. is
here to resurrect him through a point of declara-
tion in the M.E. fief which is this—all the messages of North America go up to the Brooks
Range. That land above the Circle, man, is the

land of the icy wilderness and the lost peaks and the unseen deeps and the spires, crystal receiver of the continent. Wait and hear. Goose your frequency.

★

CHAP TEN

★

Listen, did you know, creep technician, about the superconductivity of metals at absolutely low temperatures? yeah, fab, you get down at three degrees or four degrees of absolute zero (and that's *the* zero, man—lower you cannot go) guess what—there is five metals, no more, which become super superconductors. Take a ring of Thallium, that soft shit, put it at 240° abs. for absolute, run a bar magnet through the middle of the ring, run it out again, and the current that's induced won't stop running around the ring for months. So, employ your new knowledge, take a cunt, put her near Absolute Zero, work up a ring of troth (this is a wedding, you nut) composed of Old Thallium, Mother Mercury, Lemuel Lead, Timothy Tin, or Ike Indium, any one of those soft spooky witch metal elements will do, cool it till it's as cold as that beauteous cunt out near Absolute Zero, and then, man, hold your hairy jewels, cause a shock is coming up, why you just take and run and plunge your dick through the near absolute zero ring, zing into that gone ice snatch, whoo-ee! whoo-ee! pull it out before you rock stone ice pinnacle prick. You just set up a current, man, is going to keep that cunt in charge for months. Whoever said your gong was not a magnet? Oo la la, Françoise, your trou de merde is inoubliable for it is like the Camembert my mozzaire used to make when we were young, Boonkie.

Fuck this noise, why is D.J. hovering on the edge of a stall? Make your point! But D.J. is hung because the events now to be recounted in his private tape being made for the private ear of the Lord (such is the hypothesis now forging ahead) are hung up on a moment of the profoundest personal disclosure, in fact, dig, little punsters out in fun land, D.J. cannot go on because he has to talk about what Tex and him

were presented with there all alone up above the
Arctic Circle, and that's where the root of the
hangnail grows, it all happens faster in the
Arctic C, there's gathering of ionization on those
polar caps, those auroral regions are electric,
man, more ground charge than the rest of earth,
cause the messages are coming in, the M.E.F.
(Magnetic-Electro Fief—don't forget) is charging the joint by night, those ice ass pinnacles of
the Brooks Range are vibrating to the modu-
lations of the waves, a crystal oscillator is every
mountain has got ice on its tip, and there's lots
of mountains and lots of ice, pick up on this—
the boys, you will remember, dear gi...sed-out
auditor, have just finished cooking their breakfast, and aware of game all about them, half-
clean themselves from the walk, half-fouled with
the emanated nauseas of medium assholes and
Rusty high-grade asshole, disillusioned with Big
Luke's Cop Turd copping out on the big game
hunter's code and oath, and just in a general state
of mixed shit, for the walk up to here has done
them only a minim of good. They have not
cleaned the pipes, not yet. They are still full of
toilet plunger holes seen in caribou, and shattered guts and strewn-out souls of slaughtered
game meats all over the Alaska air and Tex feels
like he's never going to hunt again which is not

unhorrendous for him since he's natural hunter,
but then with one lightning leap from the button
on his genius belt to the base of his brainpan he
gets the purification ceremony straight in his
head, and announces to D.J. that they gonna
wrap their weapons and lash them in a tree, and
then they going to walk through the forest and
up to the peak with their Randall bowies, and
their binocs, and packs, but nothing to protect
themselves with except the knife. They each
know even as he says it that this is how you get
the fear, shit, disgust and mixed shit tapeworm
out of fucked-up guts and overcharged nerves.
But D.J. is in a grab for your dick competition
snit that he didn't think of this first, so says,
"Let's leave the Randalls behind, too."

And Tex replies, "A man can't go without a
knife."

"Do it or don't do it," says D.J., "but don't
finger fuck yore ass."

Man, this is striptease shit. "Then we don't
take our binocs," says Tex.

"Then don't take our packs."

No sleeping bags.

No food.

No compass.

Man, they got some of that mixed shit out of
them already. About the time they cache all

belongings, they own clean fear now, cause they going to live off the land. And they as light as if they lost gravity. D.J. could take a ten-foot spring. If it wasn't cold ass this morning, he'd be ready to go naked. Oh, that country looks big and mean up ahead.

But they got to take a backward step. Cause their ass is freezing half to death. You ever count on the weather in Brooks Range, kiss your own fever blister, mister (you know how you got it) that weather is like a bitch with hot and cold water running in her bush. Right now it's running icy shock cold. They push up not two hundred yards after we left them caching their gear, going through the boreal-montane, not two hundred yards through a forest getting skinny in its Arctic birch and alder, hardly a black spruce left, and squat, they at the edge, they at timberline again, and the ridge of the hill they been climbing is there, bare, twenty yards ahead of them, and they top that, and look down on a long valley, more forest, and then ahead to the beginning of a range of snow-topped mountains, bare-ass peaks, bare as the bald head of an egg, bare and white as the crest on a wave, and more mountains behind them, and more behind, like an arrow across the morning blue shooting for two hundred miles or more across mountains no

man ever saw from the center, only from the air,
and nothing but snow, even now in September
nothing but snow, land as white as a desert and
deserted, just peaks. And it rings back at them
like a stone on a shield, no, better block that
metaphor, drop it altogether, Lady Ethel, it rings
back like a finger wet on the rim of the best piece
of glass on Park Avenue, New York, yeah—D.J.
ain't been East for nothing—those mountains are
a receptacle, man, a parabolic reflector, an avatar,
a bowl of resonance, listen to the boys totter just
at the icy look of them, and they know they got
to go back a little on their newfound principles,
they got to take a bedroll and grub, their pup
tent, the matches, a rope, shit, they can't go
clean, they even take the binoculars, but mixed
shit does not flow in again to the reservoir of
their heart because celestial mechanics is built
on equations and going with nothing into the
forest is not necessarily more loaded with points
of valor than going with rudimentary bag and
forage yet without arms into mountain snow.
September, and that land ahead is white as a
sheet! So they still clean, and lost thirty minutes
pulling down lashed gear from the tree and lash-
ing it up again to keep grizzer from cleaning
them out before they return, but now they really
off, they up over the ridge, down into the forest

draw, and climb up again, and one hour and twenty minutes later they are on the edge of the snow, that same snow which looked to be near as an arrow shot away. But now the sun is out, and it is hot, man, up to 65° and more which is hot in that snow and the dazzle is like sunlight on the water.

"That dazzle," said D.J., pushing into the sluggish kind of mealy new wet powder, not fluff, not sludge, just a bit of going heavy, three inches deep here, no more, here at the beginning of a snowfield, one thousand miles wide (or near to that) and two hundred miles north across the mountains onto tundra again, "that dazzle," said D.J., "is like sunlight on water."

"Shit," said Tex.

"Yeah, man, it's like the dazzle on the water outside of Herod's court in Caesarea, ever hear of that?"

"Shee-it," said Tex.

"Well, you ain't no I.Q. competitor."

"Fuck, I ain't. I compete you in anything."

"Never mess with me, ignoramus."

"Why," said Tex, "tell me about Herod and his fuck hole in Caesarea. When you done I'm gone to do a Caesarea up your ass."

"You ain't seen the day you was strong enough

to unzip it out of your pants around me, pussy kisser."

"Pick the dingleberries out of your teeth. Who was Herod?"

"Herod was a royal goat fucker, you cock-sucker."

"I," said Tex, "never sucked a cock in my life, but I'm going to make you the first. I'm going to suck your cock and bite it off and send the bloody abomination to your momma."

"Oh, man, you'd be a cha-cha faggot if you wasn't so ugly."

Hey, hey, is this the way they really talk? And at sixteen and seventeen. Well, yes, they is geniuses, D.J. been telling you. And all that pederastic palaver? Hell, yes. They is crazy about each other. They even prong each other's girls when they can, but fear not, gentle auditor, they is men, real Texas men, they don't ding ding ring a ling on no queer street with each other, shit, no, they just talk to each other that way to express Texas tenderness than which there is nothing more tender than a flattened pan-fried breaded paper-thin hard-ass Texas steak. And don't forget those French fries and the dead fly in the red crud rim of the bottle ketchup, not to mention the citric acid in the salad dressing—we ain't got those gut bucket skillet flat Texas ass stomachs for nothing. Listen, fellow Americans, and D.J. here to tell you, don't get upset by the boys' last dialogue, they so full of love and adventure and in such a haste to get all the mixed glut and sludge out of their systems that they're heating up all the foul talk to get rid of it in a hurry like bad air going up the flue and so be ready to enjoy good air and nature, cause don't forget they up in God's attic, that country way upstairs, Brooks Range here, to say not too far from Mount Michelson, that's a mount, and so fret not those of ye who live for the quiet of Sunday on our quiet streets, those boys would not talk that way to your daughter or your sister, no, sir, they would just ruminate privately a little, and do their best to fuck her.

Yeah, and now they don't talk for half an hour, and just walk along climbing in the barest parts of the snow which is three inches and two and not too bad, but for the drifts where it is foot and more, and then Tex, all quiet and cool, puts a light grip of a hand on D.J., and whispers, "Shut up, now, there's a wolf on the ridge."

And that wolf is a sight. He's a white wolf and he weigh in at one hundred and plus and plus, just a long big high beast of a white police dog the size of a Dalmatian and more. And that wolf is doing nothing, he's just running along the ridge, and taking a bound now and then and his big white fur goes up in the air and separates just as lithe and quick ass from the snow. There's times you can see nothing more than a mouth, nose and eyes, black outline black as paint, two ovals, two green-gold eyes, black stub of a nose, air so clear you can see the shine in the cavity of the black nostrils, and then the mouth, black outline, red gums, red as cut-open flesh, and white teeth, fangs. They suddenly aware they got no gun, and this wolf not much beyond one hundred yards away on the ridge is alert to something, could it be them? and they raise hackles and try to hold them down, cause those hackles are transmitting waves, and oh, shit, that wolf just turned, he's putting his radar on their waves, whoo, he's zero on them, can't see, but can sense, he takes one step their direction like feeling the pulsing up of the field—what they giving off, murder or a meal? He can't determine, so here comes another step. Animal murder is near. Everything is all silent suddenly. Nature is just as timid shit as a slum street—the boys did not know before how silent silence could be, thought it was silent in the snow, but there had been sparrows, yeah, scutterings of squirrels, yeah, white snow mice, sounds all over, now none. Each of those boys rings up the voltage in their resolve, like let that fuck wolf try to come to them, and they will give him a time, they thinking of how to kick his nuts in, choke his throat, dig into his ears with their fingers, push through his eyes to his brain (that is if he is biting one and the other does the rescue) man, they're fired, and that electric fire goes off them. Two waves of murder, human and animal, meet across the snow in a charge as fantastic and beautiful as Alexander Nevsky, thank you very much, and wolf stops dead, knocked on his psychic ass, what a pity psychic struggle cut no ice with silver iodide or movies be cheaper to make: that wolf slides off them and goes ambling down the ridge, no longer leaping and swinging at how loose, hippy-dippy, juggler balls and ass he is, no, the wolf he older, he been put down, that's no good for any presumptive continuer of his own species.

But the D.J. wave and the Tex Hyde wave which Lupo II decided to slide away from has gone wave zinging into the air where Mr. Lobster with wings, Thing with a claw, E Pluribus, old man Eagle fuck, yeah old man Eagle comes a zooming down out of the air in plummet, gray feather mass, white neck, black head, black claws, black as teakwood, man, whoo-ee, what a drop, the boys they practically clapping, he

comes from five hundred feet right down like
Magnum Lightning Zero down to the back of
Lupo II who turns just in time, opens those
teeth, wheels, stands on hind feet, swings two
forelegs, left right, cuff, cuff, and M Lightning
Zero, our eagle, hereafter MLZ, thank you, splats
into a flat out, wings out, hovers, like an *eagle*,
man, wings arched and fluttering just a tickle to
stay in place above the wolf, he just gliding in
the air one spot, his claws like lightning, zap!
zap!—they miss each other, wolf and eagle, but
that opening of the wings to brake out from the
plummet when Lupo II took his wheel, turn,
and fight, oh man, it was a shock to the heart,
cause death stood out in those wings, if you'd
been a bug in the shadow of those wings you'da
called out, "Bury me clean, Armageddon is here."
And D.J. thinks just once of his dad, and eagle
story he told him and knows MLZero is going
for the eyes, and wolf he's just going for the
meal, and in comes MLZ and L II stands him off,
miss and miss, and again they try, wolf giving a
sobbing scream like, "I'm going to kill you,
mother-fucker." And old Magnum LZ he got a
screech like a den of hooknosed women when
one of their pocketbooks is missing, so it's sob
and scream, and attack and parry, come in on a
shot, brake, claw air, veer off, do a spin back,

and Mr. Wolf like a boxer picking off horseflies in the air, cuff, cuff, coot, coot, suddenly it's bull-shit and bullshit, cause they each missing the other, old eagle he staying just out of range, Magnum Z. Lightning that's all the fuck he is, Tuckerman, and finally they done, and M.Z. Lightning humps his wings and heads on down the air carrying on like a crow, and L II nomi-nating himself as winner, sets on his hind end and lets up a call which starts low, calls in all the beasty guts for miles around, tells them of the taste of fresh game, goes up higher than a coloratura into ascents of panic and power and warning and a call to the mountain ring and then tries to hit High E above High C for nothing, to show he's a virtuoso, and fails to make it, good for him, and slides all down into bronchitis again and the smell of his own shit ass wolf hide in a hole in hibernation not so far away. And the boys understood every sound of it. And if Tex had had a gun, he would have imitated every sound of it. But they don't have a gun and once again they feel just as clean and on-edge and perfect as would you, sedentary send-in-terror auditor of this trip, when you, sir, are about to insert the best piece of cock you ever mustered up into a cunt which is all fuck for you, and your nose is ozone you so clean and perfect, well, they feel-

ing like that every instant now, whoo-ee! whoo-
ee; they can hardly hold it in, cause this mother
nature is as big and dangerous and mysterious
as a beautiful castrating cunt when she's on the
edge between murder and love, forgive the lec-
ture, Pericles, but the smell is everywhere, the
boys are moving on smell, snow smell, better believe it, good here, not so good there—move
along, this is sweet, hold up, rotten shit around
the bend, some clutch of mice, no more, but
their scampering set up the wrong scratchy little
tickler cymbal along the snow fluff and make
some smell go wrong somewhere else, something
like that. Man, it's terrifying to be free of mixed
shit. And they got the unfucked heaven of seeing twelve Dall ram on an outcropping of snow
two miles away across two ridges, and those Dall
ram solemn head and light foot make their way
down a slope, heading into valleys for winter
and for feed, it's a procession, and through the
binocs they are so white and their horns, oh,
man, the underside is yellow golden rosy color
that gives D.J. twiddles in the gut (twiddles
being of course nothing but mother-of-pearl but-
terflies in cameo, Sir Lancelot) and the sun is on
that snow and space! man. You could be Cleo-
patra on a barge and twenty galley slaves, and

the sun on the water is a feather in your nose.
Olé, olé.

Then they hear the helicopter. Man conceived
of fucking in order to get fucked. There is no
doubt of that. So, off they plunge, trying always
to keep a ridge between them and the copter,
and looking for streams so they leave no track,
and already they've left a track. Well, for the
next two hours right into two in the afternoon,
it's no action, just pain, they going in deeper
into Brooks Range and Cop Turd buzzing about,
looking here, looking there, but never too far
away. And then around two P.M. he departs,
figuring, they hope, that Cop Turd finally decided the hints of trail they left might be animal.
No, that ain't it, Cop Turd must have set down
long enough to examine their steps—hell, CT is
out of gas, Al Bell with his Bell 47J is out of gas.
That all—he'll be back.

Then they discover a valley. It's for the boys,
better believe it. A bowl below snow level, maybe two miles by one mile, meadows and wood,
tundra and rock, and clearings and shapings,
could be the Colorado Rockies it's so sweet right
in the middle of the beginning of all that snow
and wilderness, tucked between ridges of snow,
and so the boys work a trail in a false direction
into a creek, back up on their steps a mile (you

try walking backward a mile) and slip into the
forested bowl leaving behind the fields of snow-
fields and see for a last sight one pale pink fox
go springing through the snow to pin a field
mouse in snow and Arctic grass, flip, flop, oops
and out, nub, nudge, you're dead mouse and a
little echo out in the air, one small sorrow. And
then some squirrels dart from the wood, run out
by the fox, coax him to chase, and go back up a
stand of black spruce at the edge of the bowl,
black spruce again after the boys thought the
biome was dead and finished. And a wing of
sparrows go rip-titting and coo-cawing after Fox
cause he can't catch Squirrel, and Fox he humps
and scratches and whines and cries, he cries, dig,
cause Squirrel won't come down to get killed.
Maybe he's thinking of the children at home on
a starve.

Man, our two little hunt boys, Killer I and
Killer II, are excruciated. They near to being
sick from the sweet they want to laugh so hard
at Mr. Egomaniac Fox—come on down, Squirrel,
be a good fellow. Yeah, they feel so good they
stop for an inst, head to head, toe to toe, and
mill it up, each taking ten good lumps to the gut.

"Hurt?" screams Tex.

"No, sir."

"Why not?"

"Cause I'm a Royal Commando, sir." And they cackle. But the moment they stop (1) the King of Mountain Peak M.E.F. shit, (2) Mr. Awe and (3) Mr. Dread—that troika—that Cannibal Emperor of Nature's Psyche (this is D.J. being pontiferous, for we are contemplating emotion recollected in tranquillity back at the Dallas ass manse, RTPY—Remembrance Things Past, Yeah, you remember?) yeah the CE of NP, Cannibal Emperor for sure, Mr. Sender, who sends out that Awe and Dread is up on their back clawing away like a cat because they *alone*, man, you dig? why, they just dug, they all *alone*, it's a fright wig, man, that *Upper* silence alone is enough to bugger you, whoo-ee, all the twiddles have turned to plummets and they don't even know from what, and then know, it's their laughing up in the silence. They turning everything on in the wrong way, and they ready to retreat. And mixed shit is ready to drop in again on the lip of their liver.

But that meadow is beautiful. Arctic flowers, more white mountain aven with yellow centers, and the tundra gone to red and yellow and berries, dwarf huckleberries, cranberries, which they eating to calm Mr. A and Mr. D and the Cannibal, Mr. Sender, and the tart comes up out of the berry, one fine vein of sugar drawn from

sour ice. And earth, taste of sunlight the senti-
mental might declare, but the troika is on them
again, Cannibal Emperor to the fore, whoa
whoa what I dread, they can but hardly breathe,
and D.J. first to dig into the dimensions of the
message which is simple, yes, direct—bear is
nearby. That is it—a bear is near. And Tex don't
argue—all in a funk without a gun, they pick a
tree, they up it fifteen feet, high as they can go,
they wait there on the edge of the meadow, the
minutes go by. And then they remember they
have left the packs behind and down they go all
shaking, up the tree they work again, getting the
packs up, and before they once more in the
upper whippy weak crack snap branches of the
black spruce like pegs, not much better to sit
on, well, lo, behold, bear, there bear, out at other
edge of the meadow and he don't see them, no,
nor smell upwind from them, they ready to
swear they smell him.

Now, bit by bit, they cool, get back cock. Because they safe, yeah, man, safe unless the branch
break, and Mr. Bear he's all right, because their
mind-ass transmitter after Awe-Dread Bombardment from Mr. Sender is chucked down to relaxed little beeps (the boys is quietened now
from being up in the Brooks Range all alone—
you in need of a great cool-out—you try it) and

because the boys are relaxed, half in soft fear, half sweet fatigue—ain't slept, remember? they just now look, and what do you think Grizzer is doing?

Well, he after a meal, man, and he like every fat ass in the world: when he eating, you could ring a fire siren under his nuts and he never miss a beat in the gourmandize, he's humping up on all the berries—they ain't been too many this season, remember?—and so he grab with a paw and hooks in about two hundred buffalo berries at a pop, and swallows, and lets blue juice and red juice run out of the sides of his black wet leather mouth, and then raises one paw in the air and wipes said mouth on his shoulder as if he imitating a weight lifter sniffing his own armpits, then griz burps, yeah, old bear burps and spits out the next mouth of berries, and then he sighs (and they chilling him with their pistol eyes, so young and up tight with trying not to breathe they could be airline hostesses serving Frank Sinatra African rock-tail frozen ass lobster) yeah, and fighting silently over who holds the binocs, and daring each other to climb down the tree and watch from the ground, and then each of them being not up to the dare, and not certain—does private honor of Texas good heart and clean shit require they touch boot leather to ground?—but

while they debating in the lowest whisper ever
heard, "You go," no "Fuck, you go," it gets too
fascinating and they just watch some more, because Old Bear has the burps, and now he out
in the tundra with his dark mahogany hide digging up sod and scrubbing at roots, and he works
at that like a gardener, digging in one of his big
mitts, bigger in plan than a volume of *Encyclo-
paedia Britannica,* Dallas edition (which is bigger than the standard edition, natch) he's all
claws in the sod and turf of poor old skinny
misery tundra, he like a rake, yeah, he just cuts
out pieces of turf and turns them over. The un-
derneath is tundra root of all variety, thick as
nerves and shoots, thick as lamp wire, thick as
your finger, and Grizzer just eats away at this
mat looking just like a roast beef hash, crust,
black and almost charred, digging into the mat
of the earth and contemplating what the dirt
and the nerve roots and the accumulated experience of the various bugborers and slugs have to
say. And in the middle of this, sitting sad and
munching slow after slowly uprooting, expung-
ing, and devouring five square yards of peat with
many a heavy sigh and one or two fine from the
heart burps, Griz suddenly decides his ass is on
an itch and he looks to scratch it, and flings
away his mat, and works his butt on the tundra,

scraping and scratching and rolling on his back,
and thumping and bumping his ass, and then he
gets up like a fat woman and walks off in a
grump to the other end of the meadow and
sidles to a young tree and takes a bite out of
the bark on the trunk about seven feet up, just
rising on his hind legs sort of lazy and taking a
deep easy bite, mean and pleasurable, like a
businessman copping a goose on a bare-ass night-
club waitress, yum! and then he turn around, old
Griz, and shove his insatiable ass against the
bark of the tree, and he rub and he slide and
he shimmy like you rubbing a Turkish towel up
the crack of your own sweet potato, and then he
grunt and lie down and go to sleep right there.

And the boys wait, ten minute, twenty minute,
the squirrels flitting, mice heads popping in the
tundra, sparrow settling on the back of Grizzer,
indeed! and a hint of the wind spring up in the
afternoon and see a white hare, hop, hump, hop,
he gone, looking like white Benny bump tail on
a caribou, and a marmot in a burrow, and a
weasel so Tex would swear, D.J. do not see it.
Then they decide to go down and keep working
downwind from sleeping Grizzer, but griz starts
to stir. And over the ridge which they can just
see through the binocs, up in snow country again
out of the bowl, is a sight they hear first and

cannot believe cause a hundred or more, maybe
many more, caribou are passing on the ridge
and that convention of antlers looks just so fine
and unbelievable as a forest on a march. And
while the boys watch they hip into a little aggregate of fact which is those antlers (known in
plural as a calliope of antlers) are a-zigging and
a-jogging and a-twigging because there are lines
of dance shaping and reshaping around three or
four caribou gentlemen known as Bull Fuck 1,
Bull Fuck 2, etc., each of them with cows and
kids, but there's a vigorish in the air, a rumble
to be heard among these beasts, they stepping
and hopping like rutting season is near, and two
of them BF 1 and BF 3 stop for a second in the
brisk September afternoon air and hunker down
their hind legs, and then give each other a clout
with their antlers like football linemen making
contact, slap, snap, sharp and fast, then they
break off like they've had a taste of goodies to
come but must go back to march route, and all
this, especially the clear crack of antler clatter,
sharp as shoulder guards hitting each other in
loud clear hill ringing echo has done one bit of
work, Grizzer he's up, he shakes, he wheels in a
circle once, twice, then he off like a bull locomotive driving up to the ridge, and busts up and
out of the bowl and makes a mad-ass charge at

the procession of caribou, and they who have
been traveling in the deep of their noncarnivor-
ous communion to new forage, new land, new
love, and winter quarters, are off now on a tear,
as are the boys, now down from the tree and
scrambling up the ridge to have a look at the
sight of hundreds plus of beast all running
silently through the snow and Grizzer after them
cutting through the middle of that calliope of
antlers scattering like fish, then regrouping out
and around Mr. Bear and taking off and they all
getting away, of course, of course, except for one
calf who stumble in fright and griz right down
on young beast and with one paw at the neck
and the other on the flank, goes in with mouth
open to rip her belly and get the living blood and
taste of live entrail, whatever that may be, whatever taste to have fat-ass Grizzer so avid ass for
it, and when calf breaks loose half for an instant,
pain springing it near to free, why, Grizzer flips
her down again and having had his taste of her
live, kills her now by slamming his teeth through
the big muscles of her back right through to the
spine and vertebrae which he crunches in two
closing his big mouth and she breaks like a stick
of wood and is there lifeless and her death goes
out over the ridge and slips into the bowl and
the afternoon takes a turn and is different having

just passed through one of those unseen locks of the day, everything is altered, not saying how.

And Grizzer he eats awhile, and paws at flesh, he feeling fat and sort of food disgusted, and then works a little half-ass at covering the carcass over, but he's not heart in it, and after a while just contents himself by taking a piss at the head, and a big bear drop of baubles at the tail, Griz like a baron hasn't learned to read or write but sure knows sealing wax, let me put my humper monicker mooney on this. And goes off, Griz #2 about as different from Griz #1 with the big eye dying that D.J. would kiss LBJ on the petoons just to have a rifle to take down Griz 2 and see how he look when he die, similar or very different as if the center of all significant knowledge right there.

The bear is gone, and they down from the tree and exploring the bowl, but modestly, stepping in the big cool, feeling clean but weak, and too sweet, sweet as caribou. Instinct take them up the bowl and onto snow ridge and there is a caribou, mother of the dead calf, and she hardly look up when she see them, she just stand with her head down and her nose on the flesh of her dead, pushing off the snow and bits of dirt Griz 2 left, and her hooves in passing and by accident go through the bear bauble old Baron Bear has left and kicks her into a fright as if hate was suddenly stinging her feet, and she circles about in a dance, but never takes her nose off as if she is going to smell on through to the secret of flesh, as if something in the odor of her young dead was there in the scent of the conception not ten months ago when some bull stud caribou in moonlight or sun illumined the other end of the flesh somewhere between timber slide and lightning there on the snow, some mystery then recovered now, and woe by that mother caribou nuzzled in sorrow from her nose while the sky above blue as a colorless sea went on and sun burned on her, flies came, last of the flies traveling over the snow and now running a shuttle from Baron Bear's pile of bauble to the nappy spotty hide of caribou mother, she twitching and jumping from the sure spite of the sting but not relinquishing her nose and the dying odor of her yearling calf and D.J.'s head full spun with that for new percipience, since could it be odor died last of all when one was dead? and took a separate route, and where could that lead his mind, for the secret of D.J.'s genius is that he pure American entrepreneur, and so his mind will always follow a lead. Never been a businessman yet wasn't laughed at in the beginning, you bet. And here was the lead about the death of odor but then, just then, a flight of cranes went over, one hundred, two hundred, so now there were hundreds and hundreds, yes, men, they could no longer count numbers flying overhead in formations of V and diamond and echelon and hovering on course, two hundred like one, and birds wrapped up in the mission to go south carrying some part of the sky in their thousand wings as if the very beginning of autumn, seed of the fall, for North America below in all the weeks to come was in the high cawing and wing beat clear up to the fanning and vibrating of reeds some high long-gone sound such as summer coming to the very end.

That was all they saw that day. They traveled over ridges, slid down new snow on slopes and went in further. A still was on them. The cranes had emptied the pocket of this territory and they moved on seeing not a tree nor an animal nor a sight but for the glaciers ahead and the loud crack of their boom in the late afternoon, and the ridgelines, the ridgelines now beginning to dance in the late afternoon with transparencies behind turns of transparency and sunlight rising up straight from the snow in lines of razzle reflection, their eyes gritted, and afternoon chill was still good on them yes, and yes, for the

colors began to go from snow gold and yellow
to rose and blue, coral in the folds of the ridges
when the sun still hit, coral bright as the underside of the horn of the Dall ram and there were
two, a couple, high again on the farthest ridge,
first animal they'd seen in hours and then they
saw one more. It was after they put up a tent.
They came to one more bowl with a few trees,
a hint of bare ground, and a crazy salty pond,
mud and salt at its edges but very sure of itself
in the snow hills like all that Northern land so
ready to declare it has a purpose when none to
be seen, and they put up a lean-to in grove of
black spruce, last black spruce this side of the
Pole, D.J. ready to swear, and lit a fire and
cooked grub, roast beef hash, yeah, beans, bread,
coffee, chocolate bar, so tired they jawed the
food like cattle plodding, and lay down side by
side drawing heat from the fire up the blankets
into their legs, boots tied to a stay overhead,
heat of the fire putting iron back into their body
like the iron and fire of faith for those black
spruce twigs and short branches and rotten punk
for start (which punk D.J. had not forgot was
from the lore of his father of whom he could
not yet think) fuel for the fire out of the soil of
this land up on the top, cold bare electric land

of North, magnetic-electro fief of the dream, and
D.J. full of iron and fire and faith was nonetheless afraid of sleep, afraid of wolves, full of
beauty, afraid of sleep, full of beauty, yeah, he
unashamed, for across the fire and to their side
the sun was setting to the west of the pond as
they looked north, setting late in the evening in
remembering echo of the endless summer evening in these woods in June when darkness never
came for the light never left, but it was going
now, September light not fading, no, ebbing, it
went in steps and starts, like going down a stair
from the light to the dark, sun golden red in its
purple and purple red in the black of the trees,
the water was dark green and gold, a sigh came
out of the night as it came on, and D.J. could
have wept for a secret was near, some mystery
in the secret of things—why does the odor die
last and by another route?—and he knew then
the meaning of trees and forest all in dominion
to one another and messages across the continent on the wave of their branches up to the
sorrow of the North, the great sorrow up here
brought by leaves and wind some speechless
electric gathering of woe, no peace in the North,
not on the top of the rim, and as the dark came
down, a bull moose, that King Moose with antlers

near to eight feet wide across all glory of spades
and points, last moose of the North, came with
his dewlap and his knobby knees and dumb red
little eyes across the snow to lick at salt on the
other side of the pond, and sunlight in the blood
of its drying caught him, lit him, left him gilded
red on one side as he chomped at mud and salt,
clodding and wads dumping from his mouth to
plop back in water, like a camel foraging in a
trough, deep in content, the full new moon now
up before the sun was final and down silvering
the other side of this King Moose up to the
moon silhouettes of platinum on his antlers and
hide. And the water was black, and moose dug
from it and ate, and ate some more until the sun
was gone and only the moon for light and the fire
of the boys and he looked up and studied the
fire some several hundred of feet away and gave
a deep caw pulling in by some resonance of this
grunt a herd of memories of animals at work
and on the march and something gruff in the
sharp wounded heart of things bleeding somewhere in the night, a sound somewhere in that
voice in the North which spoke beneath all else
to Ranald Jethroe Jellicoe Jethroe and his friend
Gottfried (Son of Gutsy) "Texas" Hyde. They
were alone like that with the moose still staring
at them. And then the moose turned and crossed

the bowl the other way and plodded through
the moonlight along the ridges of snow, moonlight in his antlers, gloom on his steps. And the
boys slept.

CHAP ELEVEN

And woke up in three hours. And it was black, and the fire near to out. They were cold. Cold, you see, with age in their bones, and Tex, shivering, dug himself out of the chill deep folds of the blanket and D.J.'s body hugging ice to ice against him. Like a thin bitter old woman, cursing ice and old age and his lazy partner and the rheumatism of future joints, Tex poked in the dark and worked the pile of other black spruce twigs and branches into the fire, his nostrils going near to drunk from the sensitivity of mucus deep in sleep being lit up by the aroma of unsuspecting pure burning resin, turpentine converging for an instant to something like opium, you bet, the planes of flame thin, not yet hot, hardly warm till he built a cage of twigs and beat the log as if he scourging indolence to cut to the live coal and reworked and remade his fire structure, tuning it, and stood before the new flame getting some of that ingredient of Alaska earth which worked once to make a tree and give it fuel to burn for his heat, so Tex stood there pulling heat from the earth, and to the side D.J. saw a wolf go easing off and sat up in bed in ice fear and reached for a pot and clanged it.

They cursed each other for a while, Tex him for staying under the blankets, he Tex for being so dumb as never to see a wolf so near, and then D.J. got up and stood by the fire, and when they both warm, they lay down again, and got calm, and felt warm and the trouble started, trouble of the simplest sort it was that profound—they could not sleep. Lying there in wilderness, for all they knew no other man for fifteen or twenty miles, the moon was on the pond, little sounds coming from that pond, fish of the North breaking surface time to time could that be, and on the ground the restlessness of lemmings and voles, and foxes no doubt and the wolf, nothing sleeping easy in this bowl around this pond. Fire, that pit of possibilities beyond the imagination

of quadruped animals, yes, the inner throat of
the active lion easier to contemplate for such as
beasts, and the silence was not a still but came
in flows and swells like the ripples of a pool,
yeah, and each sound left clouds of silence in
the trough between each echo, and they were
wired up by the mixture of fatigue, cold, and the
first good rest they'd got, and by the life of the
day they had just passed, and by the clean in
them free of mixed shit, and lying without a gun
or knife which was like traveling naked at night
now weaponless in near unmarked mountains
watching wolf and griz, mother caribou, the
cranes never forget their hearts starting to beat
at the mystery sound of a thousand cranes' wings
near enough to lift your heart out of your body,
make it fly after. So they breathing hard with all
of this, lying next to each other like two rods
getting charged with magnetism in electric coils,
the ante going up and up under that blanket,
and in the next half hour as they lay there saying not a word in an intensity of hung suspension,
like purgatory so near they are to reaching across,
fingers poised, hands up, throats near to gorging
with heartbeat, there like that over the next half
hour the Arctic lights began, Aurora Borealis was
out like she had not been out any night in September this trip and looked to begin above their

feet across the pond, North of them in a corona
of red and electric green wash and glow colors
rippling like a piece of silk and spikes of light
radiating up like searchlights, diamond spikes
from the crown of the corona going two hundred
miles up vertically into the sky while rays and
bands, curtains of light, draperies rustled, pulses
of color went up into the dark, something agi-
tated in the bend of the night, and a crackling
sound like agitation of sparks run over a run of
silk, some light was alive and spoke to them.

"What cause that?" said Tex.

"Don't know."

"Sunspots."

"Yeah, sunspots."

"Magnetic disturbance?"

"Yeah."

Silence. And they each are living half out of
their minds. For the lights were talking to them,
and they were going with it, near to, the lights
were saying that there was something up here,
and it was really here, yeah God was here,
and He was real and no man was He, but a
beast, some beast of a giant jaw and cavernous
mouth with a full cave's breath and fangs, and
secret call: come to me. They could almost have
got up and walked across the pond and into the
north without their boots, going up to disappear

and die and join that great beast. In the field of all
such desire D.J. raised his hand to put it square
on Tex's cock and squeeze and just before he
did the Northern lights shifted on that moment
and a coil of sound went off in the night like a
blowout in some circuit fuse of the structure
of the dark and D.J. who had never put a hand
on Tex for secret fear that Tex was strong enough
to turn him around and brand him up his ass,
sheer hell for a noble Texan but he, D.J., was
beloved son of perfume on the poo Halleloo and
her sweet ass was his sweet ass and so tempta-
tion made him weak at the root of his balls and
he always swelled to be muscle hard around Tex
so that Indian could never get it up his ass nor
no man living, and vibrations coming off Tex
tonight like he giving up the secret of why he
never tried to bugger old D.J., Tex who'd bugger
any punk, cause asshole is harder to enter than
cunt and so reserved for the special tool but Tex,
who never sucked a dick and never let no one
near him not even to touch, could bugger all
but was never ripe to try for D.J.'s dangerous
hard-ass soft mother's cherry although secret
unvoiced almost unknown panic for attempting
such entrance had him nipped in the groin with
a claw, but it came out in the night some tension
of waves of unspoken confession from Tex to

D.J. that Tex Hyde he of the fearless Eenyen blood was finally afraid to prong D.J., because D.J. once become a bitch would kill him, and D.J. breathing that in by the wide-awake of the dark with Aurora Borealis jumping to the beat of his heart knew he could make a try to prong Tex tonight, there was a chance to get in and steal the iron from Texas' ass and put it in his own and he was hard as a hammer at the thought and ready to give off sparks and Tex was ready to fight him to death, yeah, now it was there, murder between them under all friendship, for God was a beast, not a man, and God said, "Go out and kill—fulfilll my will, go and kill," and they hung there each of them on the knife of the divide in all conflict of lust to own the other yet in fear of being killed by the other and as the hour went by and the lights shifted, something in the radiance of the North went into them, and owned their fear, some communion of telepathies and new powers, and they were twins, never to be near as lovers again, but killer brothers, owned by something, prince of darkness, lord of light, they did not know; they just knew telepathy was on them, they had been touched forever by the North and each bit a drop of blood from his own finger and touched them across and met, blood to blood, while the lights pulsated and glow of Arctic night was on the snow, and the deep beast whispering Fulfill my will, go forth and kill, and they left an hour later in the dark to go back to camp and knew on the way each mood of emotion building in Rusty and Big Luke and Ollie and M.A. Bill and Pete and their faces were etched just as they had forseen them and the older men's voices were filled with the same specific mix of mixed old shit which they had heard before in the telepathic vaults of their new Brooks Range electrified mind.

★

TERMINAL INTRO BEEP
AND OUT

★

A ring of vengeance like a pitch of the Sara-
cen's sword on the quiver (what a movie was
that, madame!) rings out of the air as if all the
woe and shit and parsimony and genuine greed
of all those fucking English, Irish, Scotch and
European weeds, transplanted to North America,
that sad deep sweet beauteous mystery land of
purple forests, and pink rock, and blue water,
Indian haunts from Maine to the shore of Cali-
forn, all gutted, shit on, used and blasted, man,
cause a weed thrives on a cesspool, piss is its
nectar, shit all ambrosia, and those messages at
night—oh, God, let me hump the boss' daughter,

let me make it, God, all going up through the M.E.F. cutting the night air, giving a singe to the dream field, all the United Greedies of America humping up that old rhythm, turning the dynamo around, generating, just cut through that magnetism and go, boy, and God got to give it to the Greedies, cause get a man greedy enough and he got the guts to go—go, go, Gutsy Hyde—so the Devil feeding them from one side and God having to juice man from the other, and whoa, whoa, but no, it will not slow, and these messages zoom across the lands, M.E.F. on call, at night—check on this, idiot expert technologue! —the ionization layer rises, the interference is less, the radio messages go further, zoom, zoom, zoom, like pneumatic tubes going back to the lap of Hiram Hardon, President and Head of Head's Dept. Store right up there, Endicott Mountains, Brooks Range, and an hour before sunrise as all those North America shit heads stir in their sleep, digesting the messages they sent out and got back, beginning to smog the predawning air with their psychic glug, glut and exudations, not to mention all the funeral parlors cooling out in the premature morn from the M.E.F. all through the night screams and wails of corpses exhumed, excavated, flushed, sponged, spiced, finger-fucked, flayed, sewn, pushed, cut and shoved, not to mention sliced loose from their organs and petrified man in embalming juice—every undertaker worth his junked-out gunk has a secret formula—formaldehyde, do not relinquish your secret ceremonies, your treasure chests, your Paris gardens where the vestal virgins partouse in your juice, no, sir, never forget the living, the dead, and the just dead are fighting up all those square root of minus one bands in the M.E.F. mystery kc frequently kill your cycles, and as morning comes on, one hour before dawn, they are scheming in their sleep, getting practical, getting ready to get up, yawn, cough, fart, shoot a little piss, just generally fuck up that M.E.F. band, and so, friends, the ionization layer (first cousin to static in telepathic affairs) comes down again like a cloud, and intercranial communication is muffled, no mean matter, cause at Brooks Range, on the edge of the great snow-white parabolic reflector, sitting in the silent resonant electric hum of the still, there is a rub in the air like your hair on edge or coitus all interruptus with electric coils of gas in your bowel, pain in your balls, and hate in your ding, yes, discomfort as the ionization layer settles back and the hills is full of static charge. And when the shit was over in the Moe Henry and Obungekat Safari Group bunkhouse

on Dolly Ding Bat Lake and the ice pinnacles of
the Brooks Range was murmuring the word from
ice shield to parabolic vale, "m.e.f., m.e.f., roger
and out, it's morning, come in, e.m.f.," why,
Rusty and Luke and the guides and boys and
packers and medium assholes all got into the
planes to go on back to Fairbanks and led the way
into the new life smack right up here two years
later in my consciousness, D.J. here at this grope
dinner in the Dallas ass manse, given in my
honor, D.J., I thank you, because tomorrow
Tex and me, we're off to see the wizard in Vietnam. Unless, that is, I'm a black-ass cripple Spade
and sending from Harlem. You never know. You
never know what vision has been humping you
through the night. So, ass-head America contemplate your butt. Which D.J. white or black could
possibly be worse of a genius if Harlem or Dallas
is guiding the other, and who knows which?
This is D.J., Disc Jockey to America turning off.
Vietnam, hot dam.